Just the Sex:

A COLLECTION OF EROTIC SHORTS

www.alessandratorre.com

Editor: Madison Seidler
www.madisonseidler.com

I agreed to be his wife.

The agreement was clear:

1. Sex
2. Photo ops
3. No romance
The sex was easy. Everything else, hard.

The following scenes were taken from The Dumont Diaries, a full-length erotic romance.

dance.

strip.

suck me.

The first night he came in to the strip club, I had been mid-dance when Rick's hand gripped my shoulder. I glanced over, my eyes sharp, and my irritated look turned into a question. Rick *never* interrupts when we are with a client.

He leaned over, catching the glazed eyes of my client. "Sorry to interrupt, but I need to borrow Candy. Consider the first half of the dance to be on the house." His hand pulled at my arm, not allowing me an option, and I stumbled off of the man, my heels catching as I hopped and skipped to keep up with him.

"What the hell? Is everything okay?" I hissed at him, narrowly missing the sharp edge of a table as he drug me along.

"We have a high roller, up in VIP. He saw you, wants you, up there."

"A high roller?" I fought the urge to laugh. The guy probably asked for sparkling water and Rick thought he was fancy. Our club was an establishment for truckers and minivan driving dads; anybody with any taste or money took their plane to Orlando or South Florida if they wanted girls.

"Yes, this guy is loaded. He already ordered a bottle of champagne – you know that bottle of Dom we keep in the back? Plus, he has private security and came in a limo." Rick was moving fast, his hand incessantly pushing on my lower back, his words practically panting with excitement.

I allowed myself a small sliver of excitement. This guy *did* sound loaded. Maybe this night would be different. Maybe I would actually meet someone worth meeting, someone who didn't try to haggle over the price of a lap dance, or who would try and cop a free feel. Rick pulled back the curtain that enclosed the VIP section and I stepped through the curtain and had my first glimpse of him.

There are people that bring elegance to any environment. Our VIP room definitely needed some elegance, built with functionality and economy in mind: worn black couches surrounding a small stage, black curtains on ceiling tracks that could be pulled around the couches, dividing the room into four private spaces, each with a view of the pole. This man sat on a center couch, leaning back, his arms draped out and across the couch, his feet crossed casually at the ankles, a lit cigar glowing from his right hand. Behind the couch, two men stood, their features hid by the shadows, their silhouetted builds impressive. Between them, the cigar smoke drifted across the man's face, and blue eyes glowed at me, a smug smile widening as I approached.

I masked my apprehension, holding my posture straight, tits out, stomach in, a smile across my face. I walked directly to him and stopped before him. "You asked for me?"

He brought the cigar to his lips, taking a slow drag on it, his eyes raking up and down my body unapologetically. His eyes flitted to the pole, then back to my face.

"Dance."

I turned slowly to the pole, feeling the absence of Rick, the emptiness of the room. It was odd that we were alone, that no one else was in this space. Even the bouncer had left, leaving me alone with the three men. The house music was piped through this space, a DMX song playing. I strode up to the stage, gripping the pole with one hand and doing a slow spin as I exhaled, releasing my stress and apprehension in one slow breath. *You are okay. You are beautiful. You will be fine.* I rolled my neck, repeating the mantra, my long hair sliding over my skin as my head moved. I wished for the lights, the bright lights that hid everything from me. Then I took another breath and moved, gripping the pole and swinging my body up and out into the air, a swirling motion that spun the room out of focus, allowing me a brief, short moment of invisibility.

I am reckless on a pole, trusting my legs and arms in a way certain to cause damage. It is a lover I hate and I ride it relentlessly, caressing it in a sensual way that leaves nothing to the imagination. The beat moved through me and I got lost in its strength, pulsating against steel, spinning away only to return to it, my heels a blur of clear sparkle, my thoughts lost in the movement.

My bra was the first victim. One quick unclasp, the release of heavy breasts as I spun slowly downward, my legs suspending my body upside down above the hard floor. One outward fling, and sparkles and black sequins became airborne and joyful in their flight. I kept my panties on, the thin fabric the only thing between me and the pole.

When the song ended, I was panting, my eyes finally moving traveling across the floor and then up to his. Sometimes the most terrifying thing is eye contact. It certainly was at that moment, when I was exposed, bare and gasping, on the stage before him. He had the cigar in his mouth and want in his eyes. It was a look I was accustomed to, conditioned to. But on this man the look was different. Hungry and possessive, he ate me with his stare, with the blatant desire that he made no attempt to hide.

"Come here," he commanded.

I moved carefully, down the steps on the stage, my sky-high stilettos wobbling slightly on their downward descent. Then I was before him. I watched as his hand moved, adjusting himself, the hard line of his cock outline in his pants. He glanced at it, and then at me. "Suck me."

I hesitated, the look in his eyes intoxicating, vivid blue that commanded me. Then I was on my knees, my hands working the leather of his belt, the zipper of his pants. Then his cock was in my mouth, my wet lips sliding over rock hard thickness. Behind him, motionless and silent, the two bodyguards stood, their eyes forward and hands clasped.

He said little, lying back on the couch and watching me. When he was close, I felt his hands, firm on the back of my head, pulling himself deeper into my mouth. He groaned as his cock twitched against my tongue, hot wetness filling my mouth, his hand tilting back my head, his eyes capturing mine as he finished, intense blue orbs of possession. Then his eyes closed and his head dropped back, his cock pumping one final release into my mouth.

His bodyguards paid me, stepping forward and helping me to my feet, placing a fold of crisp bills into my hand. Then they left, a trio of gone, and I was alone in the dimly lit room.

"Touch yourself."

"They can see us."

"You like that?"

"Your cock. Now. Please."

The tour of Nathan's home concludes at the guest house, stepping inside an unnecessary movement since its entire interior is shown through the glass walls that make up three of its four walls. He points out the galley kitchen, the studio apartment, complete with a living room area, fireplace, walk-in closet and deluxe bath. He seems particular interested in my opinion, and I nod politely, a smile pasted on my features. "It is beautiful. You have a wonderful home."

Then, we return, back to the majestic home's great room, my eyes flickering over the two bodyguards, who now frame the door, their eyes following us as his body guides me towards the kitchen.

"Stop." Nathan's voice, commanding behind me.

I stop, standing before a large dining table, it surface smooth and, like everything else, glass. I feel his hand on my back, sliding upward and then the release as my top is undone. I turn to face him, his eyes meeting mine as he reaches back and unties the strings around my neck, his fingers trailing over my skin as he pulls the final piece that holds my top in place. I wet my lips, unsure of my words, not wanting to say what I need to say.

"We haven't discussed money yet."

"That didn't stop you from sucking my cock." He doesn't smile.

I hesitate, feeling the fabric slide against my nipples as my top falls at my feet. "I don't normally do this," I whisper.

"What, leave the club?"

"No. Full sex. That isn't something I do with clients." *And not something I am going to do for free. No matter how big your house is.* My body argued with my mind, physically pulled to the man, wanting to reach forward right now and take his cock into my hand. My mind understood the reality of my situation; my body was consumed with lust.

His eyes bore into mine, blue depths with flecks of domination in them, his olive skin bending as he speaks. "Ten grand."

I return his stare, wetting my lips as I feel his hands slide down my sides, feel them dip beneath the lace of my panties. *Ten thousand dollars.* A figure I can't turn down. Not that, at this stage in the game, turning him down is an option. "Okay." I whisper.

He yanks outward, the quick motion startling me, a ripping sound heard, and then I am naked, feeling a tickle of lace as the ruined cloth that was my panties drops to the ground between my heels, my eyes passing over his shoulder and alighting on the two men who stand at attention, watching us.

"Your men," I whisper, feeling the strength of his hands as they move over my body, gentle and caressing, my breasts the current object of their focus. His fingers spread, running lightly over my nipples, which stand to attention under his touch.

"They stay."

"But…" my voice weak. "They can see us."

His hands still and he steps forward, till my face is tilted up to his. "That's the point. I thought you, of all people, wouldn't be shy."

I shut my mouth, hold my smartass response, don't ask the questions that are burning on my lips. *Why do you need protection? Why do they have to watch us?* I think of the money to distract me, picture crisp dollar bills so I won't have to think about the two men, their eyes following our movement. The men have already seen me give him head, this isn't much different.

But honestly, sex *is* different. It's why I don't have sex at the club. I've gotten to the point where hand and blowjobs are as casual to me as dancing, though the aftermath plays havoc on my self-esteem. Sex has always been that one line I won't cross, proof to myself that I am not ruined, that I am still pure in some fucked-up form.

He leans forward and kisses me, and I suddenly don't need the image of dollar bills to distract my mind. Everything floods the moment his lips touch mine.

Soft, sweet lips. Not what I expect from this commanding man. He brushes my lips softly, my lips parting for him, immediately wanting more. A groan slips from my mouth before I have a chance to capture it. His hands move up through my hair, gripping and pulling its strands. He tastes me, spreading my lips gently with his and dipping his tongue inside. I respond eagerly, my body taking over my mind, shoving it aside forcefully as a wave of arousal hits me. His touch turns harder, his mouth more demanding and he moves me backward, my heels skittering over tile, till the edge of the table is against me.

His hands grip my ass, squeezing it roughly, one hand on each cheek and lifts me easily, setting me on the table, the surface cool against my skin.

"Lay down," he bites out against my mouth, taking one, last, torturous sweep of my mouth before he pulls off, stepping back and watching me.

I grip the glass top, sliding backward until my elbows are resting on the glass. I watch him, watch as he unbuttons his sleeves. He breathes hard, his eyes glued to mine and walks towards me, stopping a foot from the table.

I can't figure out this man. Or rather, I can't figure out how I feel about this man. He is cold to the point of being an asshole. A demander instead of an asker – expecting me to perform as instructed. But that is what I am – a hired orgasm-deliverer. Pleases and thank yous are not required, only appreciated. But despite his cold exterior, I am drawn to him, insanely attracted to him. Maybe it *is* the money, maybe it's as simple as that. More likely it is that face, those blue eyes set under thick brows, a mess of dark hair that begs to have me run my hands through it, a strong jaw and kissable soft lips. Lips he happens to know exactly how to use.

My thoughts abandon me as his fingers undo his buttons, inch after inch of chest falling victim to my eyes. In his suit he commanded respect with his strong words and unyielding eyes. Without a shirt he has my full attention, a perfect build unveiled as his shirt falls to the floor. I pull my eyes from his chest and return to his face, seeing the set of his jaw, the intensity of his eyes. Then there is the yank of a zipper, and my eyes drop.

He is magnificent, every line and muscle defined, framing a package that makes my mouth and sex water. This is the organ that I have already experienced, the one that has kept me awake at night and ended many self-pleasure sessions. I swallow as he strides over and stops before me, his eyes studying me carefully, his hand reaching out and pressing me back, 'til I lay flat before him on top of the table.

His hands touch my legs, lifting them and tugging them outward, until I am spread wide before him. He bends, his hands on my ankle, his fingers unstrapping my heel, a loud thud sounding when the platform stiletto hits the floor. Then he moves to the other shoe, my foot lifting under his hand when it is free. He grabs an ankle in each hand and places my feet flat on the table, knees pointing to the ceiling.

"Touch yourself," he rasps, stepping back and watching me, his hand settling on and gripping his cock, which juts out, swollen and hard. The knowledge that I caused that reaction, that his touch on my skin aroused him, is powerful; the vision of him stroking his cock is carnal in its exquisiteness.

I close my eyes and attempt to relax. Attempt to ignore my open legs, the view on display for the three men in the room. I touch myself tentatively, my finger sliding up and down the slit of my sex, gentle strokes that tease the sensitive skin.

"Is that what you like?" I flinch at his voice, which is closer than I expected, right beside me. I open my eyes and turn to the sound, seeing him above me, his eyes on my moving hand, his own hand moving up and down his delicious shaft.
I nodded. "Initially, yes."

"Keep going."

I close my eyes again, my fingers never pausing in their travels, moisture collecting between my lips, my fingers grazing liquid as they move slowly and leisurely over the edge of my sanity. I allow one finger to dip in, to test my readiness, and drag some of that moisture higher, to the sensitive bud that is my pleasure center, circling the skin gently. I release a low moan, the building pleasure too great to contain, and arch my back, lifting slightly off the table as my fingers dance lightly through a torturous tease.

My pussy is beginning to respond, to flex and pant, saliva dripping from its eager lips. I can feel my clit taking attention, hardening beneath my gentle swipes, each circle moving a little closer. I am a sadistic bitch when it comes to masturbation, and my body loves me for it. I give until it wants and then I withdraw, coaxing my arousal out only to deny it. It isn't until it begs, isn't until it screams for mercy that I will allow it release, the explosion sweeter and more intense the longer I fuck with its mind.

I am reminded of my situation by teeth. Gentle scrapes of teeth against my nipples, first one, and then the other. He covers my nipples, sucking them into the heat of his mouth, his tongue dancing over the rough path of his teeth, my hand reaching up and grabbing his head, gripping that delicious mess of hair and bringing his head harder on my breasts, the sensation too incredible not to savor.

He grips my wrist roughly, yanking my hand off of his head and shoving it back between my legs, his message clear. I moan in frustration, stopping the sound when his mouth returns, visiting my other breast, the combination of soft mouth and hard teeth driving me wild.

"I'm close," I gasp, my sex contracting and screaming for release, my clit one swipe away from explosion. His mouth moves between my breasts, his fingers replacing his tongue, dragging slowly and softly over my nipples, gentle and light enough to make them arch for more. His mouth, that incredible, hot machine of ecstasy, moves, traveling into the curves of my neck, and all I can think about is how it would feel between my legs.

"Come," he orders, his mouth lifting off my skin, one of his hands gripping my face and turning it to his, his blue eyes capturing mine and holding me hostage. "Come," he repeats, need blatant in his taunt, strong face.

I try to keep the eye contact, try to give him what I think he wants, but it is too strong – that final moment that my clit has been waiting for, that perfect swipe across its swollen surface has my eyes rolling back, my world temporarily going black, his green eyes disappearing from sight as my back arches and I explode in
one.
perfect.
moment.

***

I am weak, drained, my body losing all muscle function as the last tendrils of pleasure gently fades away, aftershocks twitching my body. I should be doing something sexy, like sucking or jacking or fucking that beautiful cock. But instead I am lying on the hard ass table and celebrating the incredibleness that is that orgasm.

"Get up and get on the bed in the Master. I'm going to fuck the hell out of you." His voice is hoarse with need, hard breaths in between the sentences, the order almost a plead despite the command in his tone.

I move, my limbs sluggish and irritable, my orgasm party cut short. My brain tries to process his words, tries to remember where the Master Bedroom is. I am aided by his hands, pushing me through the kitchen, down a short hall and into the first doorway, my bare feet hitting thick carpet as my eyes adjust to darkness with a rainbow of a thousand city lights stretched before me.

My body is spun by his hands until I face him, the lights reflecting in his eyes, his mouth finding mine, his hands gripping my waist and lifting me up and outward, until soft bed is beneath me and he is above me, the thick length of him stiff and heavy against my thighs. I part my legs, his body settling between them, his mouth taking my throat, soft kisses alternating with delicate feedings of my flesh, his tongue teasing and torturing the hollows of my neck.

He grinds against me, his hand reaching down and placing his cock upward between our bodies, its hard shaft heavy between my legs, every thrust of his pelvis creating delicious friction on my sex. He lifts his mouth from my neck, hovering above my mouth and changes the pace, kissing me softly and deeply as he slides his bare cock over me. I gasp against his mouth, an ache between my legs growing, the tease of his shaft driving me wild, every withdrawal thrust giving me hope that he will move it two inches lower and bury it inside of me.

I, despite my ridiculous stripper standard of abstinence, have had plenty of partners; my college career littered with drunken hookups and failed relationships. The one-night-stand experience and I are old acquaintances, having shared three or four awkward experiences. One-night stands have, in my experience, always been disastrous, two strangers fumbling through sex while trying to convince each other that they are having timeoftheirlife sex. This is something else entirely.

This is electricity, sizzling between our bodies and creating heat of intense need. There is, at this point in time, no going back. If he changes his mind, pulls off of my body, I will tackle him to the ground and take his cock. I am ravenous, my body crying out for his, my mouth, fingers and skin itching for his touch, for his domination. What he demands, I will freely give, his orchestration of our sex uncontested. I don't want to battle with him, I want to pour out my body for him to use in any way he sees fit. I have tasted submission to him and love the release of control.

He pulls off of me, disappearing for a brief moment, only to return, his hands rolling over his cock, shielding it with a thin skin of latex. I lay back, my fingers where his shaft had previously been, my sex begging for stimulation, needing a release that will only be sweet enough if he participates. My eyes devour him as he climbs onto the bed, positioning himself between my legs, his eyes on mine.

"Tell me what you want."

I don't respond and he grips my legs, pulling me to him, my legs and body open to him, his hands pushing mine away. He brushed his stiff head over my swollen lips, watching my eyes. I take a quick breath, the tease of his head too much, the look in his eyes even more of a turn-on. Possessive, dominating, with a fire behind them that both terrifies and electrifies me. He knows what I want, what I need. But I love this look in his eyes, the raw need and demand in their intensity. If withholding my response lights that fire, then I want to drag it on as long as humanly possible.

He leans forward, grips the back of my neck and lifts me towards him, till my face is beneath his, his hot breath on my lips. "Tell me," he spits out.

I resist, my eyes glued to his, my body swooning when he presses his thick tip against my soaked opening. My eyes shutter close, the pending sensation too good not to savor. Another inch, shoved firmly in, another quick intake of breathe. Holy hell. My body reacts to his in a way I've never experienced. His firm grip, tangled in my hair, grounds me – his cock causes me to soar to unnatural planes, satisfying a carnal need I never knew I could have.

"Tell. Me." He orders, his mouth against mine, close enough to touch, but just enough space to torture. He withdraws slowly, causing me to moan in anguish.

"You," I whisper against his mouth.

"Louder."

"You," I say stronger, spelling out the word as our eyes meet. "Your cock. Now. Please."

He thrusts fully, my body crying in joyous celebration as I get to experience all of him, his hard shaft causing my eyes to shut and head to fall back against his hand. I grab his shoulder, gripping the strength of him, wanting to be close to him as he withdraws. Then thrusts. Then withdraws. Long slow fucks in which my body memorizes his shape, contracts around his girth, and worships his stroke. During these minutes, he owns me, regardless of the money or the orders. I am fully and completely his.

I wrap my legs around his strong body, my heels digging into his perfect ass as he increases his pace, the slick sounds of our bodies mixing with hot breaths and rough kisses. He kisses like he will never get enough, feasting on my mouth while maintaining a fluid rhythm with his body, propping himself off of me with one hand while the other hand cradles my neck, holding me up to him.

I can't take much more of this, the furious pace building an animalistic need inside of me, a need that will only be fulfilled when I come. It is close, my core pulsing around his cock, our kiss interrupted by my gasp, my whimper as my entire body tenses underneath his.

"Don't. Stop." I beg, bucking backwards against his hand, my head rolling as the buildup reaches an overflow point, my orgasm on the edge of explosion. He releases my head, bracing both hands on the bed and unleashes the full force of his cock, quick, fast thrusts that are perfect in rhythm, perfect in speed, and heavenly on my body. I risk a look upward, at the god above me, his body framed by city lights, his face determined and intense, the muscles of his chest and arms emphasized by the position, the overall package too much. The orgasm rips through me, tearing out sensibility and logic and barriers on its path, my body tensing underneath him, my heels gripping him tightly and I wildly reach out, wrapping my arms around his neck and pulling him to me, the movement doing nothing to slow the fuck, my orgasm stretched out with every pump of his muscular hips.

He doesn't give me time to rest, rolling with me until I am on top, dizzy with lust, staring down on the beauty that is BlueEyes.

"Ride me." Dark, dangerous words, spoken with an edge.

I move, grinding my hips against him, a rolling motion that creates friction on my clit.

"No. Up and down." He scowls at me, the expression doing nothing but making whatever vibe he rocks more devastating. I move my feet underneath me, resting my weight on my feet and move, lifting up and then down, feeling him respond inside of me, his shaft thickening and straightening, a slight twitch in its movement. I groan at the sensation, the stiff rod slick and hard inside me, filling my sex with every downward path. I settle fully down, the depth surprising me, the complete fullness something I can't remember ever experiencing. His hands reach out, gripping my waist and holding me down, thrusting slightly from below, my mouth opening slightly at the new sensation, my glazed eyes held by his, a cocky smile crossing his face. He pins me against him and moves both of us upward, sliding along the bed until he is propped against the headboard and supported by pillows, sitting half up, the change affecting the angle, a delicious effect that has me shivering in pleasure.

"Fuck me." His words are strong, his eyes locked with mine, his smile dropping slightly as need overtakes his features.

I move, sliding up and down in hard bounces, the impact eliciting a smile from him, a nod of approval. I move my hands to my breasts, the movement familiar, one I do on a nightly basis during a lap dance. I lift the weight of them, squeezing them against my skin and am surprised by the change in his face. He sits fully up, knocking my hands to the side; my vertical movement temporarily paused by the action.

Moving swiftly, he grips my wrists, pinning them behind my back and transferring them to one hand. I pull with my hands, unable to free them and frown, his face now level with mine, inches away. I lean forward, trying for a kiss, wanting to calm whatever storm I have awakened, but he pulls back. "Keep riding," he rasps.

The new position forces me to my knees, my feet sliding beneath me. I obediently continue, my inner stretch indicating that my unknown foul in no way affected his arousal. He grips my wrists harder, using them as resistance, my fucks turning shallower as I move to the position he seems to want, my back arched to allow my hands to travel lower, my breasts now offered to him, his breath becoming ragged as I continue a hard rhythm on his cock.

"Perfect," he groans, holding my wrist tightly, that hand now at my ass, a firm finger escaping from the cluster of hands and pressing on the exposed pucker between my cheeks. "You are fucking perfect."

A compliment. I fight to hide my surprise, warmth spreading through my body at the words. It seems that, since the moment he walked into my life, I have second-guessed my movements, my touches, my appeal. The words give me renewed confidence and I continue riding him, a gasp escaping me when his mouth lowers to my breasts.

That thing he does, that alternation of teeth and tongue – it has a stronger effect than before, my entire body at a new, ungodly level of arousal, the buds of my breasts sensitive and crying out for the attention he lavishes with his mouth. His finger moves deeper, pressing gently on my ass until it is given entrance, the tightness causing him to swear against my breasts, the added sensation causing me to tremble.

"I can't – I'm about to..." my warning isn't going to occur in time, my orgasm impatient, seizing my body in a full attack, my legs going dumb from the assault, pleasure rippling through me even as alarms warn me to keep moving, danger of weakening this orgasm ahead.

He takes over, pants of excitement coming as he fucks me from below, thrusting in and out as he holds my body still with his hands, his finger in my ass gripping slightly as I come apart in his hands, a cry ripping out of my throat, animalistic in its strength.

I think he's coming also, grunts coming from deep within his throat, his upward thrusts hard and fast, pounding and shaking my entire body with their strength. He releases my wrists, gripping my waist with both hands and forcing my body into action, pulling me up and down in rhythm with his strokes, until he roars, a primal bellow of ownership and conquer, his strokes slowing as the sound fades from his throat, wildness in his eyes, his mouth taking mine as his hips slow, his arms wrapping tightly around my body and holding me solidly against him. He marks me as his, strokes of his tongue speaking clearer than words ever could, ragged breaths coming from both of us as our mouths separate, and then reconnect, him tasting me fully as his cock softens inside of me. Then he pushes against my chest, lifting his mouth off of me and rolls over, depositing me onto the bed and kneeling on a tangle of sheets, his bare body towering above me on the bed.

I stare at him through drugged eyes, my eyes making a slow and delicious journey over every curve, cut, and bulge of his body. The best sex of my life has officially wiped me out, every muscle a relaxed mess of orgasmy uselessness. He breathes hard, staring at me, then wipes his mouth and hops off the bed, walking bare assed out of the room.

angry.

rough.

dominating.

sex.

Nathan is a man possessed, grabbing me the moment I enter the room, his hands tight on my arm, my robe's thin silk doing nothing to prevent what will be bruises. I drop the cool exterior, the mask that I adorned before stepping into this house, and look at him in panic.

He is a ball of barely restrained emotion, his breath coming in short, controlled bursts, his face dark, the lines in his face heavy and pronounced. He pushes me, over to the leather chaise lounge, until I am on my back and he is towering over me, his hands in fists.

"Nathan, please." I gasp, moving away from him, my robe open around my legs.

"You think this is a game?" he hisses. "Our marriage, our agreement?"

I open my mouth, searching for something to say, not understanding his anger. Was this over the pool? My little ridiculous swim?

He leans closer, 'til his mouth is inches from mine, 'til his breath is hot on my skin. "Answer me."

I wet my lips. "No," I whisper.

"No, what?" he snarls, yanking the sash on my robe, the silk moving easily under his strength.

"No, its not a game." I keep my face timid, my voice soft, but inside my teeth bare and my claws flex. No, it's *not* a game, this is my *life*, my worth, my sanity. For a man who doesn't like games, he should throw out the rules and stop keeping score of who is ahead in the I'm-in-control race. His eyes are hard on mine and staring in them tells me exactly how furious he is. I have never seen him this angry, have never seen this level of emotion from him in any way. It lights a fire in my belly, knowing that I have elicited this response, knowing that he *cares* enough to be mad.

He reaches forward, gripping the back of my neck and pulling me up, pressing his mouth roughly to mine as he pulls open my robe, baring my body to him. It is not a kiss. It is a domination, strong movements of his tongue that tease, taste, and torment my tongue. He nips my bottom lip, fucks me with his tongue, then gently kisses my swollen lips, taking one final journey of my mouth before he pulls off.

I open my eyes, expecting a softer Nathan above me, expecting the change in his kiss to reflect the forgiveness that had occurred. His fists have loosened, those hands now running rampant over my body, my robe fully open, my legs parted with his knee. His face has calmed, the deep lines faded, the set of his mouth relaxed. But his eyes betray him. His eyes show the fierce anger that still burns brightly. And I know. I know that my punishment is not over.

These depths of fire flicker to the backyard, then return to me, and I understand. This is how he will punish me. Public humiliation, putting me on display while he fucks me senseless. He will remind me of where I came from, treat me like the whore that I – that one night – was.

And he does. He makes me stand, naked before the window, my palms to the glass, his hands on my ass cheeks, fucking me so hard that my breasts bounce from the impact. I feel the sting of his hand, against my ass, while his words spit out hard and unforgiving, "You belong to me. You are mine."

The landscapers, bless their hearts, keep their eyes low, focus on their work. But I know they see. They see when he forces me to my knees, his hand firm on my head, my bare body before his clothed one. They see when I take his cock deep down my throat, my body shaking from the effort, when my back contracts and I gag. They see when his thighs flex and his eyes close and he fills my throat with satisfaction.

But that's not the worst of it. The worst of it I am ashamed to say, ashamed to admit to myself. The worst is that, even at the height of it, even when I felt their eyes, and hated Nathan's demands, I was aroused. Panting in my pussy, moisture dripping down my leg, aroused. I moaned when he spanked me. I begged for more as he fucked me. I looked into his eyes and asked for his cum.

I know. I am as screwed up as he is.

forbidden.

cheating.

want.

"I jack off to you at night."

I have angered Drew. Too many questions, which is a common mistake I make. But my workout is over, two mind-crushing hours with Beth, the bitch who won't stop till I vomit, the one who thinks soy is delicious and sweat is pleasure. And I feel, as I twist the cap and chug cold water, that I should have some sort of reward, such as answers.

I don't know why the questions make the bodyguard so mad. If I didn't know better, I'd say it is the mention of Nathan that boils his blood. But if he is that easily riled up by Nathan, the man would have gone crazy by now. Drew's life spins around the axel that is Nathan, his every move orchestrated by the manicured hands that are Mr. Dumont.

My question of the day is a simple one, coming to me during an agonizing long set of sit-ups. A simple question. I ask it in the kitchen, twisting off the lid of my water bottle, the five words rolling off my tongue as casually as I can dispel them.

Drew's eyes go from disinterest to stone to anger to fury. My water bottle hits the floor, water jetting in all directions as he grips my shoulders, slamming the refrigerator door closed and shoving me against it, his face close to mine. I tense, closing my eyes to his furious green ones, taking a gasp of air before shutting my mouth, willing my questions to shutthehellup for a moment. "Shut up," he whispers, the words a growl against my skin, my feminine body realizing so many things in one brief second.

His hard body against my own, the unforgiving ridge of his muscles impressive.
The peppermint flavor of his breath, hot in my ear, yet finding its way to my nose, and I inhale his scent – a blend of grass and sweat and mint that is intoxicating.
His hands, originally against my shoulders, have moved. One is now cupping my neck, pulling my head to one side, the other grips my ass, his large hand slipping under the loose hem of my shorts and grips my bare skin tightly, fitting our bodies together in one, unending connection.

His breath, that hot air that was against my ear has moved, along the curve of my neck, his head lowering to my skin, his breaths quickening to match the fast beats of his heart, which thud hard against my breasts.

Oh, and that arousal. Hard and hot, a brand against my leg, my body twisting underneath his hands in order to put that arousal where it belongs, tight against my sex, the thin material of my shorts doing nothing but increasing the pleasure when I involuntarily ground against him.

He swears, his hand forcing my head to straighten, his mouth hesitating over mine.

I need it, I need his lips on mine, need his passion for me, I need that hard cock in more places than against the silk of my shorts. I want his fire and energy inside of me, I need confirmation that I am still woman and I am still desired. I grind again, one small movement that confirms the size of his need. He groans, his hand gripping my ass tighter, pulling me against his cock as he thrusts against me.

His mouth makes the final move and closes the distance, his mouth drinking of me in an agonized, desperate fashion.

My heart beats erratically, pumping blood in wild fashion to all of the organs that are crying out. My clit is demanding an enormous amount, my core so wet, so aroused, so needy for more stimulation. My brain is screaming, a loud, unintelligible sound that wants to know WHATTHEFUCK is going on. Then he pushes off of me, one hand moving slower than the other, his bottom hand delayed in its release of my skin.

We stare at each other, the distance between the island and the fridge too small, our bodies too close. I must look like a woman possessed – my hair wild from his hand, my lip gloss smeared, eyes needy, mouth panting. He is staring at me as if he is terrified of me, his hands gripping the granite of the counter's edge, his chest heaving. He suddenly moves, holding up his hands and moving slowly away. "Just…Christ! Just stop asking questions. Please." He moves away, a door slamming a moment later as he moves to his part of the house.

I worked at the Crystal Palace a total of three years, three months, and twenty-one days. My empty days give me time to calculate useless statistics like that. You'd think that that length of time, spent before men, gauging their level of arousal, would have taught me something. Would have taught me the difference between harmless flirting and a danger zone. Would have given me enough life experience to steer me in a direction other than the one I am in right now, which definitely feels like danger.

My hands are shaking. I hold them before me, staring at the tremor. I sink to the kitchen floor, picking up my water bottle, my eyes noticing the spilt water. I took a deep drink, waiting for my heart to calm, my hands to still, my shakes to pass. I need to get to my room, need to separate myself from him, from this kitchen. I need to take a shower, to lie down, take a nap. I stumble away from the counter, grabbing my tee-shirt, putting foot ahead of foot in a quest for normalcy. Out the door, into the guest house. Two steps inside the bedroom, I feel his hand grab my wrist, yank me around in one clean moment, and bend his mouth back to mine.

There is not a moment of hesitation in his kiss, his hands releasing me, his mouth following mine as I fall the final inches onto the bed. He moves above me, our lips moving, tongues intertwining, mouths crushing, tasting each other fully.

My confused state is gaining intelligence as I move, the implications of what we are doing ringing alarm bells in my mind. But the forbiddance, the risk of being caught, only makes it hotter. My hands scramble over his chest, fumbling down to tug at his belt, my fingers frantic in their quest to have him unzipped and exposed. I can feel him pushing out, his pants tenting, his readiness impressive.

His mouth won't release mine, the scruff of his stubble burning the skin around my lips as he takes what he has wanted, pinning me down to the bed with his kisses. And then, finally, I have him in my hand, my palm closing around a stiff shaft, and he closes his eyes and pulls off of my body.

"Wait. Take off your skirt."

I do, shimmying the fabric down and off, watching as he reaches into his pocket and pulls out a condom, ripping it open with his teeth, the intensity of his stare causing my breath to hitch and my mouth to water. I spread my legs before him, opening myself fully up, his eyes feasting on the sight, and he kneels on the bed before me, stroking the latex of the condom down his cock.

"I know what you like," he grounds out, teasing my opening with his stiffness. "I've watched you fuck so many times that I feel like I've had you. Do you like when he fucks you?" He thrust fully inside, my eyes closing at the sensation, a moan spilling out of my mouth. His hands flip my legs over, turning me to my side, his torso coming down, his mouth taking a greedy tour of my breast while he pumps his hips, his cock dragging slowly in and out, stretching me, the angle perfect in its sensation.

"Do you? Do you like his cock?"

I don't answer, pulling his head down on my breasts, gasping when his mouth takes my nipple in, sucking it, his green eyes on me, his teeth gently scraping my sensitive skin. I roll to avoid his eyes, facing the mattress, bringing my knees beneath me and arching my back, his body moving with me, his cock beginning a faster movement, pumping in and out as his hands roam over my ass and along the line of my back.

"I've thought about this for so long," he groans. "Being inside of you. I jack off to you at night. I picture your perfect mouth, sucking my cock. I think about you just like this, bent over before me, waiting for me."

I can't respond, my mind arguing with my body that this is wrong, that I should pull off of his body and walk away. But my body loves his words, loves the depth of the passion, the idea that this man wants me, has thought of me. My body loves the feeling of him inside of me, his hands which are now cupping my breasts, his mouth planting soft kisses along my back as he continues his fucks. Fast, hurried fucks, as if he is worried that I will disappear and he needs to get his fill of me first.

He is not Nathan. Our bodies do not mold in perfect synchronization, our arches and valleys do not coincide, there are times when he moves left and I move right. But he has fire for me, he cares. He is a living breathing man who has the capacity to love, who looks at me and sees something more than a contract.

He returns me to my back, his body settling over me, his mouth softer on mine, kissing me slowly and softly as his strokes bring me *there*, to the point where my mind stops thinking and I come, my breaths shuddering into his mouth, my body clenching and contracting around him, causing his eyes to shut and, a moment later, his own finish to come.

yearning.

his mouth on my most private place.

ravenous need.

The sound of the door wakes me, the slide of glass against rubber disrupting the silence enough to cause my eyes to open. I lie still, trying to decipher what has awoken me. The room is dim, never fully dark, the many windows allowing moonlight to filter through the curtains. Then the door clicks into place, and I stiffen.

I hear the gentle slap of bare feet, and then there is weight on the bed, the mattress adjusting as a figure moves across it. There is a tug on my blankets, a breeze as the fabric is lifted from my skin. Then warmth.

He moves against my back, wrapping an arm around my waist and pulling me tightly. My body slides easily across the fine sheets, 'til I am solid against his. His skin is so warm, his body so hard, his arm gripping me tightly, a hold that wraps me in a cocoon. I feel the scratch of stubble against my neck, and he burrows his face into my hair. "I'm sorry."

His whispered voice is so thick, so full of emotion and need. It matches the need in my heart. *I need this so bad.* I need to be held, be protected, be embraced. He nuzzles the skin on my neck, placing a soft kiss there before continuing. "I just … I couldn't go to sleep without touching you."

I arch against him, sliding my legs in between his, fitting my body even tighter into the curves of his. He reacts, his hands traveling, turning, and gripping me until there is not a single place on our bodies that is unconnected. There is nothing for me to say—no words for what is a terrible idea. Words will only ruin this moment. Words mean thought, and I can't think about what we are doing. I know what I need. I know what I want. And right now, in this one quiet moment, I want to be selfish.

I roll, his hands sliding and tugging to keep me close. I look into his eyes, seeing a desperation in them that matches my own. Then his eyes drop to my mouth, and I am lost. He carries such a hunger for me, his desire typically locked behind a stern, rigid exterior. But here, in the privacy of my bedroom, with Nathan's room only three or four walls away he releases it; a storm of want, his passion breathtaking in its simplicity. He follows his line of sight, lowering his mouth to mine, his hands pulling my waist to him, a strong leg wrapping around me and drawing me close.

Kissing him is so different than Nathan. Nathan and I have emotional expression in our kisses, our lips able to communicate in ways that we will never be able to verbally. Drew's kiss is so different. His eyes, his mouth, his touch, his words — they tell me everything I need to know. His kiss is more of a sexual fuel, taking this sweet, needy moment and pouring the kerosene of passion onto it. It starts off slow, the need of us both flickering in our half-asleep states. But it continues, his hands moving quicker, pulling me upright, yanking at the silk of my camisole until it is over my head and I am half naked before him. He moves to his knees, our kisses frantic, our hands twisting into each other's hair, tugging and pulling. Then I am pushed back and I feel the slide of silk against skin as my boy shorts take the long journey down my legs and off my body.

He kneels on the bed between my legs, my body naked before him. He pulls up my legs, placing my feet on his bare chest, his hands running softly along my legs, a look of drugged arousal heavy in his eyes. And there before me, lit by the moonlight, I can't help but compare them.

He is rugged where Nathan is finely cut, scruffy where Nathan is smooth. They have the same messy hair — hair that is short enough to be professional but long enough to grip in my hand and pull. His chest is covered in a thin layer of dark hair where Nathan's is smooth, his abs thicker where Nathan's are thinner, his build stronger, evidencing his strength.

I love the look of my feet on his chest; I love the contrast of my lighter skin against his darker, delicate feet against masculine strength. He leans slightly forward, digging my feet into his pectoral muscles and his hands slide down the inside of my legs, pressing gently out as he moves, my feet sliding off his chest, my breath hitching as my legs fully open, and I am spread eagle before him. His hand gently touches the silken hair that is my core.

"Drew, I …" I stop talking, his fingers sliding along my wet slit, his eyes on mine. Then he lowers his head, moving his hands to my thighs, and his eyes are on nothing but me. My face burns, and I prop myself up, about to protest, my mouth forming the words. Then I see him and stop, my mouth dropping open slightly, the view so carnal I almost moan.

He is examining me, his fingers sliding down my thighs and massaging the skin on either side of my pussy, opening and closing the lips, his warm breath tickling the skin, making every movement of my skin tickle in the most tantalizing way.

He glances up, his eyes black with need. "God, I needed this," he groans, lowering his hot mouth onto me, my back arching at the shock of his hot, wet mouth, the soft trail of his tongue as it flickers lightly over my clit, his entire mouth working in perfect coordination to bring all of my senses to that spot.

My back hits the sheets, my hands reaching out and fisting fabric, the surrender of my body to him complete, his face buried in my most private place, doing something that is too perfect, his tongue knowing — without instruction — just how gently to sweep over my clit, just how to draw me into his mouth, how to use his entire mouth and not just his tongue. That look on his face, before he buries his mouth on me, is one a recovering alcoholic gives an ice-cold beer. Ravenous need. And it is obvious, from the sounds and expertise that he is showing below, that he loves what he is doing. It is something that I will do with him whenever — holy shit. I am about to come, my back arching, the swell of pleasure interrupting my thought processes, interrupting everything within a half mile radius, so pure and intense, swelling up the hill, small whimpers coming from me as it climbs.

Then, pure silence, my body wracking beneath his mouth, his tongue maintaining the perfect flutter against my small bud of nerves until my breaking point — a point he somehow instinctively knows. As I fall down that hill of pleasure, his tongue gently carries me down, slowly, softening imperceptibly, until I sink into a sea of perfect, post-coital bliss, my world going dark, every sense leaving my body in one perfect moment.

Jello has nothing on my limbs, their loose and pliable movement easily manipulated by his hands. He moves my legs, lifts my torso, and tucks my body underneath the sheets, pulling the soft weight of a down comforter over me. I murmur words of nonsense, trying to follow his movement, his soft chuckle irritating me briefly, my heavy eyes uncooperative. A sigh of relief leaves me when I feel the blanket lift, feel his heat settle in behind me, his arms stealing around my body, his lips gently touching my neck. "Sleep Candace," he whispers.

I should be offering to take care of him. I should be rolling over, pushing him to his back and dragging those way-too-sexy sweatpants off his hard, muscular hips. But I don't. I grip his arm tightly across my chest and close my eyes, the relaxation of release bringing sleep to me quickly.

"No sir."

"Go in my office and get on your knees."

"Please. Spank me again."

Nathan has spent the day at home, working in his office, my eyes watching the glass walls, seeing him at his desk. Visitors came at noon, two men, who went over documents and then left, Nathan returning to his seat, his hands running through his hair, frustration marring that beautiful face.

I feel like a voyeur, watching him from the air conditioned perfection of my home, marveling at how I still find him sexy, his loosened tie and rolled up sleeves, the darkness on his face when he speaks on the phone.

I am getting turned on, a ridiculous side effect of boredom and Nathan's presence, and I decide to swim. I pull on the first bathing suit my fingers find and step outside.

He is a sickness. I decide that on lap twelve. A virus that I cannot combat. Despite his incredible talent at being an asshole, I want his touch, want his approval. I want a cure but fear I would hesitate to take the medication.

I come up for air and see him, standing at the edge of the water, his hands on his hips. "Get out."

I struggle with my limbs, swimming to the edge, pushing up and over the side, and stand, dripping wet before him. His eyes take in my bikini, the thin cords that run to small triangles, my breasts practically bare before him. He steps closer, his eyes flicking upward and meeting mine.

We stare at each other, brown eyes to blue, our connection unwavering as he lowers both hands to my breasts, sliding his palms under the wet fabric and squeezing. My eyes close slightly, pleasure sweeping through me, and he rubs rough thumbs over my nipples. "Open your eyes. Look at me."

I respond, opening my eyes and looking up, his blue depths studying me, noting the hitch in my breath when he squeezes, the slight drop of my bottom lip as need grows.

"I was working," he says roughly. "Working when you stepped outside. Do you have any idea how hard I get when I see your body?"

He waits for a response, my mouth moving without sound. I clear my throat, almost whispering the words. "No sir."

"Feel it. Now."

My hands move quickly, jumping into to action, anxious for what awaits them. Wet hands on expensive fabric, unzipping and unbuttoning, reaching in and grabbing impressive, hard heat. Rock hard. Ready.

He bats my hands away, pulling at the strings of my top and letting it fall on the pool deck, the sun hitting my swollen breasts, the nipples hard and aching from his touch, then steps back, looking my body up and down. "Go in my office and get on your knees. You're going to finish what you started."

I move quickly, his presence behind me, my skin tightening as I move into the air-conditioned house. My feet cover the distance, turning corners and then stepping onto the plush carpet of his office, my wet feet sinking.

"Before the chair. Kneel."

His order comes from behind me, and I do as I am told, my knees hitting the carpet, his steps coming beside me, my eyes looking up to find him staring down at me.

"Perfect," he said hoarsely, sitting down and reaching in his pants, pulling out his cock and laying it out before me. "Swallow it. Deep."

He keeps his eyes on me, watching as I run my hands over its length, wetting my lips and inching closer, trying to keep my eyes on his but pulled to the magnificent sight before me. It twitches beneath my hands, and he pulls on the back of my head, eager to have it in my mouth.

When I close my mouth on it, sliding my lips over his head, the veins in his cock swollen under my fingers, he groans. A long, slow groan of release, satisfaction. He cradles my hair in his hands, his head tilted, watching me suck, watching my eyes close as I gag, the width and depth of him too great to take.

"Fuck," he swears. "Do you know how often I think about you at work? Think about you just like this, behind my desk? I get fucking hard thinking about you." He pushes my head harder, sitting up slightly and watching the slide of his cock intently.

His cell buzzes, on the desk, and he reaches for it, his eyes never leaving mine. He answers the phone, pulling at my head, his eyes ordering me to continue.

I love the taste of his skin. How hard he grows in my mouth, the moments when I taste the sweet drops of his arousal. There is nothing that turns me on more than having him before me, his hands urging me on, his most sensitive organ twitching underneath my tongue. I work my hand over his length, pulling him from my mouth and moving below, taking his balls into my mouth, and rolling them along my tongue, his words pausing in their speech, a brief hitch in his tone.

I smile, skimming my teeth lightly over the skin, watching his eyes close briefly, his mouth struggle to return to the conversation, his words halting when they come. I return to his cock, sucking with renewed energy, my hands and my mouth working in a wet, sexual tandem.

He stands, pulling my head back slowly, dark eyes watching as inch after inch of his cock leaves my mouth, my cheeks hollowing from the suction, my tongue teasing and flicking as he pulls me off. "John. My wife needs me. I'll call you back." He ends the call and tosses the phone aside, pulling me to my feet in one quick movement.

"Bend over. In my chair. Right fucking now."

He yanks at the strings of my bikini bottom, pulling it away before I am in place, my knees hitting his chair a moment later. It is a wide leather chair, worn and sitting low, my knees putting me at the perfect height for his entrance. He pushes a finger inside, swearing when he feels my readiness. "Is that from this?" he asks, thrusting inside, my insides tightening around him, anxious for every inch of his entry. "Does it turn you on to suck my cock?"

I nod, knowing that it won't be enough. Knowing that he will want more, will want to hear my voice. I want the reaction my silence will bring. He slaps me, the hard, rough impact against my skin causing me to jump, to moan, the possessiveness of the contact causing a curl of pleasure to shoot through my body. "Answer me."

"Yes." I gasp. "Please. Spank me again."

He waits, fucking me hard, the percussion of our skin quick, the anticipation of his touch causing my legs to tighten, my core to grip him tightly. It is building, my mountain of lust, my body shaking and breaking around his stiff rod, each thrust perfectly timed, the entire act too erotic for me to take. Being fucked like a whore, I am learning, turns me the fuck on. Then it comes, hard, open hand slaps, against my skin, his fingers gripping after each contact is made, each stinging stroke taking me closer and closer until

Ecstasy.

My body breaking into a thousand splinters of
pleasure, a series of gasps spilling out, my back
arching and pushing against his hard pelvis, our
bodies joined as I am torn apart in a sea of desire.

I love two men.

I fuck two men.

They are both aware that I have another.

The following scenes were taken from Sex Love Repeat, a full-length erotic romance.

curl of pleasure.

spread open on his lap.

I am your dirty little slut.

My men are so different, yet similar in so many ways.

Their eyes. A similar tint of blue, but Paul's smile at me with carefree abandonment and Stewart's pierce my heart with their dark intensity.

Their bodies. Paul's naturally muscular, his arms developed from hours of surfboard paddling, his abs ripped from balancing on a board, his thighs and calves strong from jumping, balancing, and kicking through currents. Stewart's body, attacked like everything else in his life, with fierce devotion, aggression worked out with miles on a treadmill, weight lifting, sit-ups, pull-ups, and calisthenics.

Their love. Paul loves me with unconditional warmth, his affection public and obvious, his arms pulling me into him, his mouth littering my body with frequent kisses. Stewart loves me with a tiger's intensity, his need taking my breath away, his confidence in our relationship strong enough to not be bothered by the presence of another man. He stares into my soul as if he owns it, and shows his love with money, sex, and rare moments of time.

Tonight is one of those rare moments. I have his attention, his cell phone is away, and he is staring at me as if I contain everything needed to make his world whole. I step forward, toward his seated form, the dress hugging my form to perfection. He sits up in the chair, spreading his knees and patting his thigh, indicating where he wants me. I sit sideways on his thigh, my eyes held by his, his hand stealing up and running lightly along my bare back. "You are breathtaking." His voice gruff, he leans forward and places a light kiss on my neck. "And you smell incredible."

"Thank you. You clean up pretty well yourself." And he does. In a suit that no doubt costs more than my dress, he looks every bit the successful executive he is. Short, orderly hair. Clean-shaven chin. Those intense eyes staring out of a strong face. "Is the car here?"

"It's downstairs. But it can wait." He runs a hand up my knee, sliding the material of the cocktail dress up.

I wait, my breath becoming shallow, my concentration focused on the path of his fingers as they travel higher, taking their time, the tickle of rough skin against soft flesh. He leans over, brushing a quick kiss over my lips and then moves lower, soft kisses making the path down the line of my jaw, whispers against my neck, and deepening in touch when they reach my collarbone. His hand caresses my thigh, the brush of his thumb moving higher until it is just breaths from my sex. I groan, sliding my hips forward, but his hand stops me, gripping my thigh and holding me still. "Not yet. Let me enjoy you for a moment."

There is the sound of approaching footsteps, and I open my eyes to see a suited man, our driver, round the corner and stop short when we come into view. His eyes drop respectfully, and he speaks softly. "Mr. Brand, I'll be downstairs with the car when you are ready."

Stewart mutters something unintelligible, the man taking the cue and leaving, the firm pull of the door behind him leaving us alone. Stewart's hands push apart my legs, moving the fabric of my dress aside and leaving me bare and open to his eyes. He looks down, examining the exposed skin, his mouth curving into a smile. "No panties?" His eyes flick up to mine.

"They're in my purse. I figured they would be useless until we got to the event."

"That," he says softly, his fingers teasing the edge of my lips, circling the edge of my sex in slow, tantalizing brushes, each touch closer but not yet *there*, "is why I love you. You know me so well."

His eyes stare at me, dark pools of lust and want. While Paul and I talk, incessantly, often, about anything and everything, important or not, Stewart and I fuck our way through this relationship, our time often too short for anything more than physical contact. Sex is how we connect — share our feelings, emotions, and love. I stare back into his eyes, my eyelids closing slightly when he slides one confident finger over the knot of my clit, that finger effortlessly sliding down and into me, the small invasion a tease of perfection. "Look at me," he breathes. "I want to see your eyes."

I reopen my eyes, my mouth parting as he cups my sex, slipping a second finger in with the first, both of them working together, stimulating me in their movement, his thumb staying firm on my clit, soft pressure that moves slightly with each stroke of his fingers. He watches my eyes, sees the moment that the fire of my need hits them, sees the crescendo and burn of my arousal, adjusting the pace and pressure of his fingers in accordance with my want. I feel the curl of pleasure, growing in my belly, our eyes caught in a web of want, pulled to each other, my eyes barely noticing the sexy pull of his mouth into a smile as my breathing increases, and I thrust into his hand. His other hand steals around my waist, sliding up my chest and pulling on the fabric there, tugging my neckline down 'til a breast is exposed, his hand grips and tugs on it just hard enough to make me gasp.

"I want you like this forever," he whispers. "Spread open on my lap, your skin in my hands, your pussy hot and tight around my fingers. You are so fucking beautiful."

I buck under his hand, my heels finding the floor and pushing off, my hand sliding up his pant leg, desperate to feel the heat of him in my hand before I come.

Blackness.

My eyes shut, and I moan, my legs convulsing around his fingers, the strum of his thumb on my clit softening, whisper soft, stretching out my pleasure as I moan over and over again. When it fades, when it softly pulls delicious heat from every area of my body, the need grows. Intense, animalistic desire, a craving for every bit of him in every place on my body. My eyes snap open and find him watching, a curve already in place across that sexy mouth, his hand on his open fly, pulling out the object of my desire and stroking its hard length against my bare leg.

I push his back against the chair, stepping over his leg, straddling his waist and lowering myself down, my sex so wet it drips, my need so great I moan. His hands catch me, carry my ass down, impaling me with his cock, his own groan sounding in the large room, his eyes darkening as I tighten around him. "God, you were made for me."

"I'm your dirty little slut," I whisper, sliding up and down, my heels firm on the ground, his hands tilting and pulling my ass how he likes it, in a way that causes my clit to hit his pelvis, the tight squeeze on my ass pleasurable in its slight bit of pain.

"You *are* my slut," he grounds out. "You need my cock."

"So bad," I agree. "I can't get enough of you."

He thrusts from below, pulling me down, the extra depth causing me to gasp, my body to grind, the pleasure shooting a spike of arousal through my core. "Tell me you love me."

"I love you."

"Again." He thrusts, sitting up, looking into my eyes, our faces inches apart as I look slightly down on him.

"I love you," I whisper, gripping the back of his chair.

Then his eyes close, and he leans back, sliding his hands up and tugging the other side of my dress down, exposing both breasts to his hands. And I know what he wants. I know, just like I know every inch of his body, exactly what he wants. I lean back, my hands resting on his knees, my back arched, my body open before him, and fuck his cock. Pumping up and down on his so-hard-it-will-break shaft, my legs carrying my body, his eyes opening and skimming greedily along my skin, his hand reaching forward and lifting the hem of my dress, strumming the bead of my clit until I come — body tightening, mouth screaming, world exploding.

Then he takes over, leaning forward and scooping me into and against his chest. My legs wrap tight around his body, his cock stiff and slick inside my sex, he carries me over to the wall, presses me up against it, and holds me there with strong arms. Then he thrusts, over and over again, whispering my name softly, and then louder, 'til he comes with a massive groan, his legs shaking beneath him, my own wobbly when he lowers me to my feet. He keeps me there, pinning me against the wall with his body, my breasts tight against his tuxedo, his hands stealing into my hair, his mouth soft and sweet on mine. Drinking from my mouth, tasting me, taking his time, inhaling my scent.

"I missed you this week. I needed that." His voice is gravelly, thick with satisfaction and truth. He tilts my head up, looks into my eyes, then lowers his mouth back to mine.

"I want him to fuck you in the powder room while I sit here with these stuffed shirts. I want you to come back to this table with your cheeks flushed and his cum inside of you."

Two hours later, my fingers steal under the tablecloth. Reaching over and gripping Stewart's leg, my fingers deftly slide up his thigh, his hand catching mine, eyes shooting a questioning look in my direction. He coughs gently, breaking eye contact as he glances to the woman on his right. "That's correct, Beth. With quarterly projections where they're at, there should be no need for additional debt. If anything, we should capitalize on our current assets." He listens to her response, his hand firm on mine, keeping me at bay. But I *need* him. I need to feel his strength beneath my hand, to feel his arousal in my grip. When the conversation turns away from him, he leans over, plants a soft kiss on my neck, and whispers in my ear. "Do you need something?"

"Yes. You. Now." It is an unfair request, one I shouldn't make, but I am panting for him. I will not make it through this four-hour dinner, through the polite chitchat that will follow, cigars in the men's club while I sit with dignified wives in the front parlor. I need a release, need firm hands digging into my skin, his mouth on mine, cock inside of me.

He studies me, a war going on behind those eyes, his glance flitting around the table and then down at his watch. He leans forward again, close enough that I can smell his scent, the masculinity crawling across the table and robbing me of rational thought. He grips my wrist, pulling my hand tightly and places it on his crotch, brushing his lips against my ear as he speaks. "Call him."

I pull back, confused, his hand cupping the back of my head, keeping me close to him, my eyes studying the tumultuous depths of his blue. "What? Who?"

"*Him*. Call him. Have him take care of you. I can't leave."

There is only one *Him* in our life, our world comprised of three people. I try to process his words, spoken without anger or light, in a serious, I'm-not-fucking-around tone. I shake my head, his eyes sharpening at my reaction, his hand pushing my own down on his cock. His voice rasps in my ear, thick with arousal and authority. "I want it, Madison. I want him to fuck you in the powder room while I sit here with these stuffed shirts. I want you to come back to this table with your cheeks flushed and his cum inside of you."

I feel the twitch of him beneath my hand, see the flicker of excitement in his eyes, and realize the truth of his words. "Seriously?" I whisper, almost afraid to voice the question.

He slides my hand up, letting me feel the hard ridge of his arousal. It is pushing at his pants, his excitement unquestionably hard. "Call him. Now."

I sit there for a moment, the hum of conversation muting as my mind processes this new avenue. My need moans between my legs, its intensity doubled by Stewart's words, by the twitch of him that proved his sincerity. Can I go there? Can I bring these two worlds so close and still escape with our dual relationships intact? I excuse myself and step away, pulling out my phone, watching the dark gleam in Stewart's eyes, a sexy smile crossing his lips. He is serious. He wants me to be fucked while he sits a few rooms away, surrounded by wealth and business. I dial Paul's number, biting my lower lip and step farther away from the table, holding Stewart's gaze.

"Hey babe." Paul's voice is lazy, as if he'd dozed off on the couch.

"Come into town. The W Hotel in Hollywood. I need your cock."

A minute later, I return to the table, smiling demurely at Stewart, who rises at my entrance and pulls out my chair, his napkin hiding any erection he may have. Leaning down as he pushes my chair in, he softly speaks. "Is he coming?"

"There are so many places I could go with that question," I murmur. "But yes."

He sits back down, reaching for his wine glass and smiling at me. "Good."

I try to pay attention to the conversation. Try to eat my salad and smile politely, nod appropriately, laugh when the overweight man to my right makes a joke. But I am waiting, my leg jiggling nervously. Waiting for the buzz of my phone against my leg, for the moment he is here. My call surprised him, his soft voice hardening when he heard my directive. I could imagine him sitting up, trying to put the pieces together, hearing the raw need in my voice. He knows me as well as Stewart does. Knows that when my blood rushes and need hits me, there is only one thing that can satisfy it. Cock. Thrusting roughly, taking my body as its own. He knows I can't contain it, that the need grows and expands until my fingers or someone else's body fucks it to sleep. He knows I won't want to make love. He knows I will need my brains fucked out, and he knows exactly how I like that done. As Stewart does. They have memorized my body, learned my tells, fucked me enough that every movement is delivered before I have to ask.

I am brought back to the present when I hear Stewart speak, his expression calm and intelligent, the rough scrape of his voice only visible to me, who knows it so well. I can see the slight tighten of his jaw, can see the fire in his eyes when he casually glances my way. He is aroused and allows my hand to confirm it when I reach over. Full-blown, hard as a diamond, aroused. It confuses the hell out of me and makes me wet at the same time. Then my phone buzzes, and I am out of time to think. I stand, gripping my purse, waving the men off as they start to rise. "I'm sorry, I'm not feeling well. I'm going to step outside for a bit."

False concern crosses Stewart's features as he rises, excusing himself and escorting me to the door. "You will be the death of me, you know that?" he says softly.

"I could say the same for you."

He stops, outside the door. "Have him fuck you hard," he bites out, pulling me into his body with sudden aggression. "And whatever he doesn't take care of, I will. Just give me a few hours to finish up this business. But hurry." He slaps me on the ass, hard enough to sting, my panties soaked at the forbidden nature of this entire experience. I grip my purse tightly and step out of the restaurant, into the hotel lobby, and head for the restroom.

I knock gently on the unisex door. "It's me." My voice croaks on the last word. This is the closest my two worlds have ever come to colliding. Stewart and Paul. In the same building. My dark and my light. My dark, now seated, surrounded by finery, listening attentively to talks of profit and loss, his cock hard, hidden underneath fine linens and discussions of intellect. And my light, swinging the door open and pulling me inside, slamming it closed behind me and flipping the latch. No words spoken, his hands thrust me back, his mouth greedy on mine as he tastes champagne on my tongue, our need thick in the air. I reach for him, my hand running down his worn tee and grip the top of his jeans. He has not changed clothes since I saw him last, has not dressed up for his entrance into this hotel, and I love the contrast. His messy hair to Stewart's combed. Five o'clock shadow to clean-shaven. The smell of sweat to cologne. I normally get a cleansing period, the twenty-minute drive between my worlds clearing my head, my skin, my palette. Now, walking instantly from one to the other, the comparisons are overwhelming. He pulls back, releasing me. Wiping a hand over his mouth, his eyes take a slow tour of my body.

"Look at you," he whispers. "Dressed up like you are a good girl." He hasn't seen me like this. With my hair conservative and a cocktail dress on, pearls at my neck. He slides my dress up, the expensive fabric stiff, staying where it is put, the black peep of lace panties exposed. I stay still, my back against the wall, legs slightly forward and spread a few feet apart. My chest heaving, need gripping me, I watch him unzip his pants and pull out his cock.

"Suck it. On your knees in this bathroom. Suck my cock while your boyfriend sits at the table."

There is an edge to his voice, an anger that is not normally present. An emotion that turns my easy-going Paul into something darker. *Sexier.* I love it, love the bite in his voice, the possession in his hand as he grips the back of my head and pulls me fully onto his cock. He thrusts into my mouth, his eyes on mine, the connection between us unbroken as he fucks my throat, growing with every pump, the fire in his eyes making the need between my legs almost painful in its intensity.

I pull off him, gasping for breath, his arms pulling me to my feet before I even speak, his arm pinning me to his body as his other hand wraps around, slides underneath the edge of dress and squeezes my ass. Hard. So hard I gasp, his eyes tight on mine and he releases it, running his fingers down the crack of my ass and fingering the channel of my sex, covered in lace. His fingers run back and forth over the spot, a grin stretching across his face at the dampness there.

"Is that for me or him?"

I don't answer, reaching between our bodies and fist his cock, wrapping my hands tightly around it, every vein in the organ outlined in the rigidity of his arousal.

"Answer me, Madd. Answer me while I fuck you right here. While I make you scream so loud that people walking by will hear."

"Make me," I whisper, a challenge in my tone.

His hand tightens around my waist at the words, his eyes holding mine with a fierce look as he listens to my words.

"Make me scream your name while he conducts his business. Make me your slut, right here and now, and send me back to him with your cum dripping out of me."

He groans, pushing me back against the wall, spreading my legs with his knees. He reaches down with both hands, grips my panties and pulls, ripping the sheer fabric with one strong jerk. Then his body is back against me, his chest hard to mine, his bare cock rough and bobbing at my entrance, pushing for and then finding the wetness of my sex and pushing inside. "Jesus Christ, Madd," he groans, shoving upward, his hard thighs pinning me to the wall, his hands yanking at my straps, pulling my cashmere cardigan off my shoulders and jerking the top of my dress down. He thrusts again, his thighs relaxing and then flexing, every fuck bouncing me back against the wall, his hands clasping my breasts, squeezing them into his palms.

"Make me scream," I grit out, my eyes on his. They are tortured blue, cloudy with arousal, latent with need. "You know that he fucked me? Before we came here. I straddled his cock and rode him. His hands rough on my skin, his cock taking my body. He was inside me, Paul, right where you are now." He roars, his voice raw and primal, pushing me against the wall, losing control as he slams against me, faster and faster, until my body becomes a shaking sea of desire, my core rattled, breath gasping, his thrusts urgent and dominant, his breath ragged, his hands finding my face and bringing my mouth to his.

"You are mine," he guts out, pumping into me, the length and level of his arousal brutal. "Mine," he swears, as he releases my mouth and turns me around, pushing me forward as he yanks my legs back, one hand hard on my back, the other gripping my ass. He doesn't slow the movement, giving me full, hard thrusts, my breasts bouncing from the top of my dress, the mirror above the sink giving me a full view of my slutdom.

Paul, in worn jeans, a white t-shirt, light hair mussed, mouth open, intensity over his face. His reflection pulls at my hair, tilting my head back, and I find his eyes on mine in the mirror.

"You like what you see?" His words are terse, thick. He is conflicted, but—from the level of his erection—fully aroused at the same time, his speed increasing, his breath loud in the small space. "You like being fucked while he's in the next room?"

I don't answer, my climax too close, every muscle in my body tightening in anticipation of the act, throbbing and contracting around him, his eyes closing briefly at the sensation.

"God, Madd. You are so fucking good …" He pulls out abruptly, leaving me gasping, my chest aching as I turn to him, feeling his hands before I fully move; they shove me back, wrapping around my waist and lifting me, setting me on the low counter of the sink, and pulling me to the edge. He jacks himself, looking at my pussy, at the swollen pink lips of my sex, then glances up to meet my eyes. He steps forward, pressing himself at my base, pushing my chin up when he sees me glance down. "Look at me. Look at me and tell me what he did to you. Tell me what he did, and make me come all fucking up inside of you."

I close my eyes at his first thrust, the angle different, better, in its brush of my g-spot. "He sat me on his lap, in this same dress. Those panties? The ones you ripped to shreds? I wasn't wearing those when I first saw him. Because I knew he'd take me as soon as he could." He pulls out of me, my eyes catching sight and gluing to the image of my wet lips sliding around his cock. His hands tighten on my ass and he pushes deeper, dragging his cock in and out of me in long, deep strokes. My voice catches at the look in his eyes, the intensity of his arousal. All playfulness is gone. This man before me — he is Stewart, but with different features, their similarities never more present than right now, and I gasp when he fully buries himself inside.

"More," he groans. "Tell me more."

"I came from his fingers, my juices all over his hand, I came and I screamed his name when I did it. I told him how fucking perfect he was and how much he turned me on." His strokes roughened with my words, increasing in speed, his competitiveness lighting a fire in my belly, and I was suddenly there again. On the brink of orgasm, need running through my limbs and pumping loud in my heart. "God, Paul, you have no idea how good his cock feels in me. How deep he goes when I straddle him and fuck him hard. How he whispers my name when I take every inch of him."

He roars, pulling me to the far edge of the sink, thrusting deeper and harder than he ever has, his mouth roughly taking my own, his tongue marking, branding, and drinking from my mouth. I push against his chest, my own body breaking in his arms, the orgasm whirling through me, my words tumbling out as I shudder with pleasure in his arms, his pace never slowing, his cries joining my own, the hot spread of liquid pumped deep with his cock, his name repeated over and over as he finally, with one final shuddering thrust, empties himself inside me.

***

Five minutes later, I slip back into my seat, Stewart barely pausing in a lengthy explanation of market trends and their expected impact. But I feel his eyes on me, see the casual glance at his watch. "Impressive," he murmurs, tugging my hand to his lips and placing a soft kiss on my knuckle. "I take it you are taken care of?"

I feel drugged, heady with the release and the knowledge of what I have just done. "Until tonight," I whisper.

"Oh, have no doubt," he says, staring into my eyes. "You will need every bit of energy for it."

I hide a grin behind a long sip of champagne, turning when I feel a soft hand on my arm.

"My wife tells me you sell books," the man says, a polite smile on his face. "Tell me, what authors do you enjoy?"

I smile politely, responding to the man, and feel the rough heat of Stewart's hand, sliding up my dress, and hear his intake of breath when he finds my lack of panties.

touch.

need.

gentle.

fullness.

My wet dress feels like an ice pack by the time we stumble, shivering, up the steps to our home. Salt water dripping down, hitting the tile and pooling, my steps careful, a slip eminent.

"Come here," Paul whispers, adjusting the thermostat, leading me into our bedroom and pulling me close, rubbing his hands over my arms, stealing a quick kiss as he yanks at his shorts and drops them to the floor.

Wow. Anyone who thinks water causes shrinkage has never met this man. At least, not this man at this moment in time. He is, despite the smile he shoots me, raring to go, and I am suddenly warm, my skin tingling, the heat between us erasing anything else.

"Turn around, baby." His words are soft, but I hear their directive and meet his eyes, a curl of pleasure shooting through me at the look in them. Raw need. A fire burning behind his cocky smile. This is the Paul I know, the one who expresses love best through touch, and who can barely contain his emotions in this moment.

I turn, hearing him blow into his hands, feeling the warmth of his skin as he pulls at my dress, his hands gently lifting the wet material off, his fingers lingering on me as they trail down my arm, as if they want every bit of me they can get. A hand tugs at my zipper, pulling it slowly down, his hot breath on my neck as he exhales against my skin, planting a soft wet kiss there, my panties the next victims to his sure and unhurried movement.

He stays close to me, unclasping my bra, his hands sliding down my back and then curving around my sides, slipping under my limp bra and cupping my cold breasts, squeezing them, pulling my body back against his chest, the hot line of his arousal hitting the top of my ass, hot to cold, my body greedy for more contact against his skin. He kisses my neck from behind, whispering my name as his hands explore my front, running over the lines of my stomach, the curve of my breasts, the hard tips of my nipples. I am suddenly needy for him in ways I have never been, needing to know that this is real, that he is mine, and we have made it through this experience intact, the proof of it hard against my backside, and I want it, him, now, in every way that I can have him. His touch slides lower, and I moan, pushing my ass back against him as his hands gently cup me, his mouth taking a delicious line across the hollows of my neck.

"Madd, I never ... you have no idea how much I love you," he groans, grinding against me, his hands holding me in place as he pushes the hard ridge of himself antagonizingly close to where I need it.

"Please," I whisper. "Paul, I need to feel it. I need you inside of me."

"In a minute, baby." Instead, I feel his fingers, their gentle exploration over and across my sex, and I push against him, groaning when they finally move inside, slowly sliding in and out, their maddening length and width not enough for what I need.

I moan, my legs weakening from the delicious touch. "Please," I beg.

He rasps, his voice thick at the nape of my neck, his arm wrapping around and hugging me to his chest. "Tell me, Madd. Tell me that you need my cock."

"I do," I pant. "I do. Please. Give it to me." My legs buckle as he crooks his fingers, brushing them back and forth over my pleasure spot.

"Only me," he says firmly, brushing his digits in a way that makes me moan. "Come to the thought of my cock," he whispers. "Then I'll show you exactly what it can do."

I do. I push every thought of Stewart out of my head, physically feel as they leave my body, and focus on Paul — my love — focus on the stiff head of him that is sliding between my legs, inches from where I need it most, so hard that it is sticking straight out. I close my eyes and think about every time he has made me moan, how his face looks when he loses control, the fire in his eyes when he watches me come. The images take me …

over the edge …
back arching …
stars forming …
pleasure ripping tingling paths through my body …

Paul's fingers keep up the rhythm, the perfect
pressure and tickle across my g-spot, every swipe
bringing new life into my orgasm, until I finally
sink, held up only by his hands, and look over my
shoulder, into his eyes, my drugged vision putting
him in a haze, a haze of gorgeous blue eyes and five
o'clock shadows.

"Fuck me," I croak, and his eyes darken, a devious
smile of carnal possibilities sweeping across his
gorgeous face.

"Yes, ma'am."

He pulls me to my feet, making sure I am steady
before releasing me. I start to turn, to face him, but
he stops my movement. "Face forward. Grab the
foot of the bed."

I obey, placing my hands on the footer and arching my back, pushing my ass out and waiting, the heater blowing warm air against my skin, my nipples hardening, my legs clenching. He runs a finger over my sex, dipping inside and then continuing up, until he reaches the tight pucker of my ass, circling the spot. Tight, hard circles, pressing against the hole until I moan, the spot resisting, too tight to allow him entrance. "Please, Paul … I need you."

His finger moves, sliding back down, taking the temperature of my sex once again, hot wetness confirming my arousal, dragging that liquid higher, soaking my asshole, his thumb replacing the finger, a bigger, harder push, not yet inside, but enough to make my breath catch in my throat.

"Tell me," he says softly, each word feathery gruff, his thumb pushing harder, breaking the seal and entering my darkest place. "Tell me how you want it."

"Hard," I whisper, my senses on full alert, wanting, waiting for what is coming, all of my arousal knotting and expanding from the intrusion in my ass. He pushes harder, deeper inside me – a gasp, followed by a moan, spilling out of my mouth. I grip the footboard tightly, feeling the collection and drip of moisture in my pussy.

"Are you mine?" His voice is tight, guttural, and I smile despite myself, waiting, tense and excited, and coming apart when I feel the width of him, pressing against me, teasing the opening of my body.

"Answer me," his hoarse voice demands, and I hear the raw edge of desperation, his need for confirmation as great as the throbbing in my core. His thumb moves slightly, pushing and then pulling, the hard sting of his hand taking me closer and closer as his finger continues its wet exploration, heat building in my ass, my mind becoming delirious from the sensation.

"All yours, Paul. I — oh God — love you." The words tear from my mouth, my pussy clenching as my ass contracts, every muscle on high alert, loving the feel of his hand as he squeezes and grips my ass.

"God, you are beautiful," he bites out, sliding his fingers into me, dipping them in and out, giving me two, then three fingers, my core tightening around him, prompting a groan to leave his mouth. "Are you ready for me, Madd?"

"Now," I blurt out, the orgasm close, pleasure rolling toward the waterfall edge that will be my flight. "Please, I need you." It is coming, a giant black hole of pleasure and his thumb pushes deeper, the dirty feel of him there so wretchedly hot, pleasure sensors go off around every inch of his thumb, his wet erection hard against my skin, his fingers sliding further, deeper and deeper, slight pain mixing with pleasure, dominance with love. I tilt back my head, *can't hold it any longer*, any coherent thought dropping off as I dive off the edge, into my orgasm, into a perfect black sea that grips my entire body and explodes it into a thousand shards of pleasure.

It is then, while my world caves in, while I am mindlessly oblivious to anything but my own ecstasy, that he shoves fully inside of me.

Fullness. The long, hard ridge of him inside me, branding me as his own, his need as desperate as mine. One hand still on my ass, his thumb making the tight fit of his cock even tighter, his other hand gripping my waist, holding me firm and letting loose on my body with his cock. He doesn't ease into the rhythm, doesn't give either of us time to react. He just dominates me: hard, firm fucks that bury inside with every stroke, a furious rhythm of domination, his breath fast and loud, my name ripping from his lips as he takes me as his own.

We are one combined machine, pistons pumping, lubed and swift, perfectly fitting as it should, no pause in our movements, no hitch in our step. He works his thumb in my ass, pushing and pulling, the tight fit glorious in its intensity. I am going to come again, the shaking of my body, the feel of two holes filled, the animalistic fever of Paul, a man unleashed, the level of his possession so fucking hot.

"Tell me, Madd," he gasps, the hand at my waist sliding down, gripping the sore skin of my ass and forcing me on and off his cock. "Tell me that you are mine."

I can't. I can't respond because my eyes are too tightly shut, my body racking underneath him, pushing harder, greedier against his skin, needing every stroke, every fuck, every inch of his thick cock as I come, a bundling outpour of muscles flexing and contracting, a scream coming from my throat, his hands loosening as I release the sound, my body growing rigid, his fucks continuing, his own climax close.

When I come up for air, I tell him. I tell him how I have always loved him. How he has always had my heart. I look over my shoulder at him, at his beautiful face, hair mussed, eyes vulnerable as he meets my eyes, relief spilling into those blue depths of perfection. He suddenly slows his strokes, the moment changing, and rolls me over, pulling out long enough to lift me onto the bed and settle down above me. He takes my mouth, kissing me deeply, murmuring soft words of love as he spreads my legs with his knees, and enters me again, slower this time, fully thrusting in and then pulling out, his eyes on mine.

I pull him to me, wrap my hands around his neck, lift my mouth to his. And I tell him, in between kisses, how deeply I love him. How I will never leave. How I am his for as long as he will have me.

His breathing slows, his kisses deepen, then he closes his eyes, thrusts deep, and comes.

my two loves.

threesome.

I awaken to the sound of my cell. It rings, the sound
dulled by sheets and pillows, and it takes me a
moment to place my surroundings, to identify the
ring. I grope through the bed and answer the call,
our conversation short, a few I love yous and then a
goodbye, his voice muffled, the signal poor as
Stewart boards the plane.

I roll back over, the room dark, and wait for sleep to
come. Minutes tick and I only grow more awake,
frustration growing with each passing moment.
Finally, my hands itching and legs squirming, I
close my eyes and let my fingers move, traveling
lightly over my body and slipping under my boxer
shorts, the cotton band yielding easily to my hand,
my fingers sliding along the thin strip of hair,
moving more, my legs spreading, knees bending,
my body quivering as I gently run my digits lightly,
so lightly, over the lips of my sex. I keep my eyes
closed and let my mind wander to my favorite
fantasy, the one that takes me quickly to the edge
and down the cliff that is my orgasm. It starts much
as it normally does, with me on my knees, both of
them before me.

Stewart wipes his mouth, his eyes on mine, piercing blue that mirror the man to his right, the man that unbuckles his pants, slowly, his fierce gaze pulling my eyes, my stare traveling from one man to the other, from one possessive glower to a second. Paul's belt buckle clinks as it is undone, and his zipper is pulled down, his hand reaching in and pulling the object of my desire out. He is beautiful, standing there, his t-shirt stretched tight over his muscular frame, his jeans low and unbuckled on his firm hips, his hand wrapped tight around his shaft.

Stewart moves, walking slowly around my still frame, stopping behind me, his hand brushing the back of my neck as his fingers find the pull of my dress zipper. He unzips me slowly, my eyes held by Paul's, as he strokes his cock and watches, his eyes dark.

Stewart's hands slide the loose straps of my dress down, and I am suddenly before them, my breasts swollen, my nipples hard against the rough lace of underwire cups, the cloth of my panties pleasurable when I squirm against them. Stewart pulls me back against him, his hands cupping my breasts, his firm fingers massaging and squeezing, Paul lets out a soft groan when Stewart's mouth comes down on my neck and his fingers tug the lace of my bra down, exposing my breasts to Paul's eyes.

Paul steps forward, his hand continuing its slow, steady movement, my eyes drawn down, and I focus on the delicious glimpses I receive, his hand exposing and then cover the rigid, stiff length of his cock. He bends slightly, his soft wet mouth taking an exposed nipple, his tongue lightly running over it before sucking it gently into his mouth. Stewart's hands slide lower, over my panties, and he firmly grips my hips, rocking me back against his body, his arousal hard against my ass. I moan when I feel it, his breath catching against my neck.

Paul releases his cock, it landing with a heavy thud against my stomach, both of his hands moving to my breasts, his hands reaching around and unclasping my bra, his fingers covering the area where Stewart's just were. Then he kneels, his mouth making a wet trail down my stomach, his teeth grazing my skin, biting me gently as he moved.

They switch places, Stewart's hands returning to my upper half, his hands turning my face to the right, and he kisses me softly on the mouth as his hands strum lightly over my breasts, lifting and squeezing the skin, pressing them together, my nipples sensitive, each brush across their surface causing me to gasp, to quiver, my legs weak.

Paul's mouth is soft and hot, his fingers skimming my panties down, down my legs, the wet cloth leaving spots of arousal on my thighs, his mouth, his firm tongue, following the path of my hair. As soon as my feet lift and move, discarding my panties to the side, he lifts a leg over his shoulder, his breath on my delicate folds, his tongue following this path, dipping into my sex, flicking over my clit, his entire mouth taking my sex in one, delicious, cover.

I sag, his shoulder supporting my weight, his hands holding me up while he buries his face into me, moaning, Stewart's cock replacing his mouth, his hand tugging me down until I am bent forward, his hips thrusting into my mouth, the firm shaft moving thickly down my throat. I gag, and feel Paul's hands tighten on my skin, holding me in place, the delicious strum of his mouth on my pussy making me lose all focus on Stewart's cock, my movements sloppy as my body grips, an orgasm close, my eyes closing as all sensors in my body tune in to his mouth. Stewart pulls me up, his wet cock sliding out of my mouth, my eyes opening to find him looking at me, his cock in his hand, the possessive look on his face on I know well.

It is the look he always gets when he thinks of Paul with me. When he thinks of another man's hands on my skin, mouth on my sex, cock in my body. The incredible blend of want and arousal, competition and conquest, that burns through his eyes and causing him to unleash holy hell on my body. Hell that feels incredible, our sexual energy uncontainable, the combustion of two bodies moving in slick, perfect percussion. And now, in this fantasy, I finally have them both. At the same time, their possessions at peak points, directly competing to bring me pleasure.

My fingers dip inside of me, cupping my sex, borrowing moisture and dragging it up to my clit, my fingers starting a steady circle around the pleasure point. I lift up slightly with my hips, my eyes opening and focusing on the dresser's mirror, the dim reflection showing my open legs, my hand moving between them. I pull off my shirt, running my free hands gently over my breasts, imagining Stewart's hands on them, the scruff of his cheeks scraping them.

Stewart tilts my face up, stares into my eyes, and I struggle to maintain eye contact as Paul's mouth takes me closer and closer to orgasm. My leg shudders around his neck, pulling his mouth closer, my pelvis beginning to thrust into his mouth as I grip his hair. "Come, baby. I want to see your face when you come. Come all over his face."

I whimper, squeezing my eyes shut, fighting the sensation, Stewart's hand puts pressure on my chin, and my eyes burst open as it comes, a swelling surge of pleasure, my mouth making animal, guttural sounds as I come, arching my back and staring into Stewart's face, his handsome smile curving in approval as he strokes his cock faster, And as soon as I finish, when my moans subside to heavy breaths, he guides his cock back to my mouth, and I work on his cock, sucking and pumping with my hands, as I feel Paul move my legs, putting me on all fours, and preparing for entrance at my rear.

My eyes flip open, my legs shaking, and I watch my body twitching, my toes curling, the reflection showing my face, flushed and panting. I forgo my clit and thrust fingers, in and out, fucking fast, my pelvis lifting off the bed as I finger fuck myself to orgasm. It is strong, racking my body, and I clench every muscle I have, the thought of Paul fucking me onto Stewart's cock stretching out my orgasm... the waves of pleasure making me moan and thrash in the sheets until there was nothing left to hold onto. I still, spent, my fingers wet and sticky, Stewart's scent on the sheets all around me. I roll over, pressing a button on the wall, the fan starting to spin about me, pushing cool air on my naked skin, a sudden chill coming over me. Reaching down, I pull the thick down comforter up, over my chest, and relax back against the mattress.

Thirty seconds later, pleasure aftershocks still flickering through my body, I am asleep.

I didn't know what I was getting into with Brad De Luca.

Didn't realize that I was stepping into a sexual world I wouldn't want to return from.

The following scenes were taken from End of the Innocence, a full-length erotic romance.

**"He understands that a ring on your finger
doesn't exclude him from the party."**

I leaned over the bar and scanned the bartenders,
trying to catch someone's attention so I could order
a drink. It was a futile effort, everyone else seeming
to capture their attention easily. I began waving my
arms like an idiot, a twenty-dollar bill in my hand.

"Come on." Brad's voice was in my ear, and I
turned, my arms still moving. "I've got us a table.

"With a waitress?" I raised my eyebrows, not
wanting to lose the headway I may or may not be
making in the 'get the bartender's attention' foot
race.

"Yes. Come on." He tugged on my waist, his large
hands encircling it and pulling. I gave one final look
at the oblivious bartenders and then turned to
follow him. We moved through the dark club,
bodies everywhere, the hum of voices and music
creating a blanket of energy.

New York truly was a city that didn't sleep. Two-
thirty in the morning, and the club showed no signs
of slowing, the energy around us ramping up with

each additional song pumping through the speakers. My mind wandered to our hotel room, six skyscrapers over, to the weekend bag already alongside expensive new purchases. Forty-eight hours in this city seemed enough time to spend a fortune and party our asses off.

I grinned down at Brad, who relaxed back on a leather loveseat, a table before him with a chilled bottle on ice. "Looks like you had better luck than me." I carefully navigated around the table until I was settled in next to him on the leather seat.

"Don't be too impressed. I had a little help." His head tilted to the left and I turned, my gaze pulled upward.

Dark blue eyes stared out from a gorgeous face, beautiful lips curving into a smile. A black suit, paired with a black shirt, hid a body that was no doubt perfect. I felt the stranger's hand tug gently on mine, and he leaned over and placed a soft kiss on my knuckles.

"It's a pleasure to meet you, Julia. My name is Marc." He gently returned my hand, and I struggled to speak.

"Nice to meet you." My words came out raspy; I swallowed and tried to regain my composure.

Smiling politely at him, I turned back to Brad, a question in my eyes.

He chuckled. "Julia, Marc and I have a long history. He was the prior owner of Saffire, but was generous enough to part with it."

There was a deep laugh behind me, and I turned to see a perfect white smile split Marc's face. "Generous? Your offer gave me little choice, my friend. But you have done very well with it, and I applaud you for that." His eyes twinkled at me. "Have you been to Saffire?"

I blushed. "Yes. It is impressive. You did a wonderful job."

He scowled good-naturedly. "It's taken a few steps upward since my name was on the title. But Rain, this is my baby." He spread his arms to indicate the club. "Unless …" he said with a sly look to Brad, "you intend on adding it to your list of assets."

Brad laughed, curving his arm around my waist. "No, Marc. I don't have the time for anything but this woman right now."

"Yes, I was admiring your ring, it is beautiful," Marc said, his eyes dipping to my left hand. "Congratulations seem to be in order. You must be quite a woman if you tied down this stallion." He sat on the closest chair, his eyes returning to mine, a knowing smile playing over his features.

"More than you know," Brad said, squeezing my side gently and passing me a flute of champagne.

I smiled without comment, taking a sip of the cool bubbly.

A man appeared, bending over to speak rapidly in Marc's ear. His gaze on me, I saw the moment when his eyes changed, urgency darkening their blue depths. He nodded and the man stood, taking a few steps back.

"I apologize, but something needs my attention." Marc stood with an apologetic smile. "Please enjoy the champagne. I should wrap up this issue in the next hour or so. Brad, if you both are interested, I often entertain in the upstairs suite. I would love to share a few drinks with you later."

Brad nodded, reaching out to grasp his hand. "As always, it is great to see you."

I extended my hand, but Marc moved closer, planting a soft kiss on my cheek. "It has been a pleasure," he said softly, the scent of his cologne lingering as he withdrew.

"Thank you for the table."

He flashed that perfect smile and then left, the strange man in his ear, quick words speaking urgently as they disappeared into the crowd. I leaned back into the crook of Brad's arm and sipped the champagne, glancing around the club, a sea of sequins, flirtations, and sexuality.

"What'd you think of Marc?" Brad's eyes held a hint of mischief.

"He's a little intense. Working hard that Rico Suave vibe he's got going on." I took a sip of champagne and looked out at the crowd.

"Did it work?" Brad's voice was low and dangerous, and I turned to see him watching me closely, a hint of a smile playing over his mouth.

"What do you mean?"

"He wants to fuck you," Brad said matter-of-factly, leaning back in the seat and tipping his glass back, his eyes on mine.

"What? No he doesn't."

"I assure you, he does. You didn't see his face when you walked up. How his eyes drank in every inch of you."

I shrugged, fighting the shot of pleasure that traveled through me. "Whatever."

"You don't understand." Brad lowered his voice, moving his mouth to my ear, taking a soft bite of my neck, then playing his tongue lightly over the spot. "It isn't just a desire of his. It is a possibility. One that he recognizes. He is like me, Julia. He goes after what he wants. And he understands that a ring on your finger doesn't exclude him from the party."

My mouth dropped, and I leaned back, putting distance between Brad and myself. "You *told* him? About what we've done?" I narrowed my eyes and Brad laughed.

"Easy, princess. I haven't told him anything. But I've known Marc for over ten years. We have run in similar circles, have shared women several times, sometimes several women." I felt a small bit of jealousy at his words, at their past, which didn't, in any way, include me.

"You've … seen him fuck?"

"Yes." He took a swig of champagne.

"And?"

"And … what?" His eyes danced with humor.

I groaned. "Don't make me spell it out. Is he …
good at what he does?" I leaned closer, giving
permission, and felt his hand return, sliding around
my waist and pulling me tightly to him.

"He is very good at what he does."

"Better than you?"

He shrugged. "Maybe you should find out." His
hand grew rougher, squeezing my skin
possessively, the change catching me off guard, a
sharp intake of arousal stealing all breath from my
body.

I bit my lower lip, and stared into the flute of
champagne, remembering Marc's lips against my
hand, and the intensity of those dark blue eyes.
"Well," I said, swirling the flute gently between my
fingers, "then maybe we should head upstairs."
Then I tilted the glass back, letting the bubbles of
champagne pop and slide down my throat.

***

An hour later, I straddled Brad's body, and he
leaned back into the sectional, his eyes drugged
with arousal, watching me, the line of his mouth
barely affected by the smile that lay there. He ran
his hands freely over the front of my dress, dipping

inside my low and loose neckline and cupping each breast in turn. "God, you are beautiful."

I said nothing, only gently moved against him, feeling a slight vibration run through us as the bass rocked a particularly loud note. I could feel the energy of the club, the muted hum of music, of a thousand bodies of barely-contained madness — dancing, kissing, falling in love — underneath us.

"Kiss me," he commanded.

I shook my head with a smile. "No. Keep touching me."

A second hand joined his first, both palms sweeping up and cradling my breasts, the pull of the fabric joined with the rough skin of his palms temptingly perfect. He growled, low in his throat. "Like this?" He squeezed, a little rougher on my nipples, my breath catching.

"Yeah."

"Then kiss me." He bucked up with his hips, throwing me forward, his upper body lifting, his mouth looking for mine, but I turned my head, gave him my neck, giggling when he nipped it.

"Not yet," I whispered. "I'm not going to kiss you until his cock is deep inside of me."

His hands tightened on me, and he groaned my name as he tore at the straps of my dress, pulling the fabric from me, a shiver running through me as my upper body was exposed.

There was a click of a door handle, and my breath caught as I looked up, seeing the black door swing open, a tall suit of gorgeous stepping inside, a phone at his ear, our eyes catching onto and holding each other.

Click. The door shut behind him, and I froze, aware of my bare skin, Brad's mouth making a wet path down my neck, his hands pushing me into place, arching my back as he traveled over my cleavage, flipping his tongue gently over and then sucking my nipple into his mouth. I gasp at the sensation, my eyes still stuck on Marc, and watch as he smiles, ending his call and tossing the cell aside, plastic on granite, a sliding sound fading into nothing as I watch him step forward, down the steps, into the sunken living room, his legs carrying him behind the couch, 'til he stood in front of me and looked down. "You started without me," he said softly, a bit of accent coating his words. Then Brad did something with his mouth, something on my nipple that made my body squirm, need growing, and I dropped my head back and broke eye contact.

Brad leaned forward, laying me back, his hands replacing his mouth. "Do you want a blindfold?"

"No," I gasped, opening my eyes and propping my body up, meeting his gaze, my stare flicking to the man standing behind Brad, his hands resting on the couch back, his eyes meeting mine. Dark blue fire. A confident smile. So much like Brad in so many ways. It was strange to have my eyes open, knowing the man I was looking at was about to touch me. To fuck me.

There was a soft slap of fabric as Marc removed his jacket and tossed it onto the sofa, fabric hitting leather, his hands unbuttoning and rolling back his sleeves. I watch his hands, avoiding his eyes, my cheeks warming, bashfulness overtaking me.

"Nervous?" His voice was quiet, a tinge of playfulness in their tone.

I looked up, meeting those dark depths. "A little."

"Don't be. I play nicely. Plus," he said, looking over to Brad with a smile, "I'm scared of the big guy."

"As you should be," Brad spoke from underneath me, settled back down on the couch, his eyes on me, his hands running over my skin, over my breasts, rough then soft, perfect patterns that kept my nipples hard and my cunt wet. "She is my everything." I smiled, looking down on him, his mouth tilting up, asking for, then receiving, a kiss. *Damn.* So much for that game plan. But I couldn't stay away from his mouth. It fit too perfectly on my own.

I saw, out of the corner of my eye, the man move. Walk to the bar, fix a drink, then move closer. I glanced at him, saw him watching me, his hand moving down for a quick adjustment before he sat next to us on the couch, but down a few feet. He reclined back against the leather, taking a slow sip of his drink, the clink of ice cubes registering to my ears. Brad pinched lightly at one of my nipples, drug my attention back to him. I leaned down, gave him a long kiss as his hands roamed me, strong drags of fingers across my skin, possession in every inch, every touch. He lifted up slightly, his hands pushing down my hips as he ground into me, the friction of his arousal causing my eyes to close, a small moan to slip out of me.

"Get on your knees. The ottoman."

I looked back, understanding Brad's directive when I saw the big leather ottoman, one that acted as a coffee table. I slid off him, letting him lean forward and drag the furniture piece over until it was flush with the sofa. He spread his legs slightly and pulled out his dress shirt. Unbuckling his pants, he drug down the zipper. "Your mouth. Come here, baby."

I climbed onto the ottoman, getting on all fours, my hands helping to pull his cock out, everything in the room disappearing as I lowered my mouth to him. I loved to suck his cock. I loved the taste of it. It tasted of need. Of raw, animal want, and never failed to cause a twinge in my stomach, a weight of arousal in my sex. I pushed him down my throat and felt him harden in my mouth.

I was caught off guard when a firm hand closed around my ankle.

***

I opened my eyes, my mouth full, and met Brad's eyes. They stared into mine, no hint of a smile, nothing but raw possession in their depths. This is the animal Brad, my favorite side of him, a side I only see in these moments, when he is watching me with another, and every alpha male instinct is on high alert. His mouth moved, curved into a reassuring smile, but his eyes were dark. Aroused. I could feel his level of want in my mouth, hard and ready, his hand settling on the back of my head and pushing down. "Take it all."

I wouldn't. I couldn't. But I took as much as I could, feeling, all the while, the slide of Marc's fingers over my skin, his weight as it settled onto the ottoman behind me. Felt his hands slide up my leg and gently work the ankle strap of my heels, careful fingers working the shoe off. Thud. One hit the floor, my foot released, his hands moving to the other. Thud. Then my feet were bare, free, and his hands were on the move. Sliding up my leg, the doggie-style position giving him a front row view to touch, travel, and then — *gasp*, his tongue caught me off guard — *taste* my skin as he moved up my legs and gripped my ass.

***

He wasn't Brad; he couldn't compare, the condom was an additional irritant, but the man could fuck. Holy hell, could he fuck. And from the glimmer in Brad's eyes, he loved my reaction. I laid on my side, on the bed, Marc kneeling between my legs, his cock quick and fast, thinner than Brad's, but hard as a diamond. He played rough, spanking my exposed ass cheek, the first hand laid, ten minutes earlier, light and questioningly, my grin and nod urging him to continue. Now he slapped my skin with aggression, the rough fucks taking me closer and closer to where I needed to be. I looked at Brad, his legs spread, still fully dressed, settled into a chair, his bare cock upright and fisted, his palm slowly stroking its length. Dark playfulness in his eyes. *Why did I ever wear a blindfold?* Jesus, the look in his eyes … I'd get on my knees and scrub the kitchen floor naked if it would bring on that look. An intense heat, possessive and aroused. I cursed any moment that I missed out on it. Just a glance at it, and I was soaked.

Brad stood, his cock at attention, forcing its way through the hang of his button-up shirt. He stepped over, climbing onto the bed and knelt before me, bringing his dick to my mouth, letting me have a taste of it before he sat back on his heels, stroking with his left hand, slowly and purposefully, just inches from my face.

His right hand played over my breasts, squeezing, teasing, then traveling up to my neck, wrapping a firm hand around it, not enough to choke, but enough that I paid attention, my pussy tightening around Marc's cock.

"Fuck Brad, she's gonna make me come." The man swore out the words, his fingers digging into the meat of my butt, one finger stealing over and putting pressure on the pucker of my ass.

"Don't stop, she's close." Brad leaned down, kissed me, deep and hard, his hand on my neck, my eyes stealing a glimpse of his cock. He lifted off my mouth, his hand tightening slightly. "God, you're beautiful." He turned his head to Marc, keeping his eyes on me. "Faster."

Marc obeyed, giving me more, harder. Exactly. What. I …

Fuck.

I took a gasp for air, getting one final look before my world went black, and I came on Marc's cock.

Moments later, I tasted the man's completion — hot and wet in my mouth. Brad finished the job inside of me. With Marc leaving us alone, Brad's hard body above mine, one hand in my hair, his kiss on my lips, I wrapped my legs tightly, felt his shudder, and celebrated one more loosening of my sexual strings.

The blindfold. I didn't need it.

semi-private.

coming apart.

in his hands.

We ended the tour in an upper-level VIP room, seated at a private alcove that looked down upon the club. Janine killed power to a small video camera that looked into the space, and we sat down around a cocktail table.

"When will the changeover take place?" she asked, leaning forward and meeting both of our eyes.

"I've already transferred the stock certificates. Scott Burge, an attorney from my firm, will send over an operating agreement for you to sign. You should receive that this week. Once that is complete, I will be completely out."

She glanced at me guardedly, hesitating before speaking. "Julia, I've never been very good with tact, so I'll come right out with this. Brad and Evelyn have left me alone, occasionally visiting the club and having monthly conference calls to discuss finances. I'm not used to having a boss, and that isn't something I am particularly interested in."

Brad started to speak, and I silenced him, touching his arm lightly. "I plan on having the same level of involvement as Brad. I am not familiar with Saffire and have little to no experience in the business world. Brad says you are an excellent operator, and I trust his judgment. Assuming we continue or improve the current level of revenue, I see no reason to get involved in your business."

Her features relaxed noticeably. "I would appreciate that. Do you have any other questions I can answer while you are here?"

I couldn't think of anything she had missed during the last hour. I shook my head and glanced at Brad to see if he had any thoughts.

He leaned forward, speaking, "I think we're good, Janine. I'll join in on the call next week with Julia, so we can touch base then. Look for that package from our firm."

She nodded, moving quickly to her feet, her eyes already roaming the club. "If that's all, I'd like to get back downstairs."

"We'll stay here and chat for a bit," Brad said, throwing an arm over the back of my chair.

"Just turn back on the security cam when you're done." She gave us both smiles and left, moving at a quick pace, speaking into a mouthpiece as she moved.

I let out a breath, turning to Brad with a smile. "She's nice."

He scoffed. "Did you expect her to be a bitch to her new boss?"

My mouth turned up slightly. "I thought we just clarified that I'm *not* her boss."

"I never treated her like an employee, despite the majority ownership I held. I'm sure you will follow suit."

"You know I will."

Then his eyes changed, from friendly to dark, and I knew, before he even lifted a hand, what was coming.

I felt the tug on my chair as Brad pulled me close to him. He captured my face in his hands, his eyes examining my features. "I love you so much," he murmured, his eyes moving over and focusing on my lips before he tugged me to him, taking ownership of my mouth with a few soft swipes of his tongue. I opened my lips further, deepening the contact, my hands stealing into his hair. I broke the kiss, pushing my chair back and standing, moving closer to him and spreading his knees with my legs. He slid deeper in the chair, reclining back against the soft leather, gazing up at me with a latent dominance of the nothing-but-trouble variety. I grinned playfully down at him, and slid one strap, then the other, of my dress down, dragging the fabric until my bare breasts were exposed, lit softly by the blue-gray lights of the room.

He groaned softly, a guttural sound, and stared into my eyes, tightening his knees against my legs. "Come here."

I shook my head and knelt, running my hands softly up his dress pants, past his muscular thighs, until I reached his belt. He watched me, his eyes darkening and he leaned forward suddenly, snagging my chin and pulling it up, his eyes grabbing me possessively before kissing me hard, a deep kiss that reclaimed his power before he released me, leaning back and watching me.

"Do you always have to be in control, Mr. De Luca?" I purred the words, unbuckling his belt with one motion, then rubbed my hand over the zipper line, feeling the outline of his cock underneath the fabric, the shape of him hardening under my fingers. He didn't answer, his eyes locked on mine, dark orbs of sexuality. I suddenly needed to see him, needed to have his bare skin in my hand, to feel the throb of what was mine. I looked away from his eyes, focusing, and unbuttoned and unzipped his pants. Then, he was in my hand, an impossibly thick, hard shaft, the skin hot beneath my palm. I stroked it, the firm grip eliciting an intake of Brad's breath.

"Put it in your mouth." The order came through in a drugged tone, desire glowing at me from under heavy eyelids.

I shook my head, increasing the speed of my stroke as I watched him. He frowned slightly, lifting his hips a bit, bringing the nine inches of insanity closer to my face. I spoke, my tone a mixture of dominance and bite. "What is your plan with the girl?"

He sat up slightly, his eyes opening more, and watching me carefully. "What girl?"

"The stripper. The one you fucked last time you were here."

"I thought that didn't bother you."

I hissed. "It didn't bother me *last* time. Things are different now. Are you going to talk to her?"

"I feel like this is a test of some sort …" he mumbled. His breath hitched a bit as I squeezed his cock, loving the feel of complete stiffness in my hands. "What is you want, Julia?"

I ran my tongue lightly, teasingly, over the top of his head, taking it into my mouth for one brief moment before I pulled off, my hands never pausing in their movement, a quick pace that traveled his entire length with every stroke. "I want you to handle it," I said firmly. "I want her to understand that you will never have sex with her again."

"Never?" I released him, the sudden departure causing his eyes to open and a frown to settle over his features. "I'm joking. Don't stop."

I resumed my movement, my free hand gathering his heavy balls in my hand, squeezing him softly as I stroked his length with a firm hand.

"Come here," he said, sitting up and pulling on my arms.

"No." I fixed him with my sternest look, my hand increasing in speed.

"Julia, come here. I want to talk to you about this without being tongue-tied by your hands on my cock." He pulled harder, his strong arms lifting me easily onto his lap, despite my best attempt at resistance.

Sitting on his lap created a new set of problems. Mainly him, standing at attention against my thighs. I sat sideways on his lap and spread my knees slightly, my hand stealing in between my legs to grab him.

He relented, shifting slightly so I would have better access and turned my face to his. Stole a kiss. I leaned back against his chest, my tension releasing slightly. His hand ran lightly up my thigh, gently, slowly moving toward the silk wisp of fabric that comprised my panties. "Are you trying to distract me, Mr. De Luca?" I breathed, my body tightening in anticipation as his second hand joined in, stealing up my stomach until it hit the exposed skin that was my breasts.

"Never," he said, his fingers caressing the silk of my panties, sliding over and over the triangle of fabric, my clit awaking underneath his touch, under the slow, perfect swipes of his fingers. I shifted, tilting my pelvis upward and pushed his hand down, letting out a soft moan when his fingers hit the place where my panties became practically non-existent. He stroked that spot, leaving the thong in place, his thumb strumming a steady rhythm over my clit as his fingers stroked my wetness. I moaned again, pushing on his hand, waiting, needing more. My eyes found his cock, heavy and thick against my leg, and I panted at the sight of glistening moisture at its hard tip.

"You're not going to get this subject to go away with sex," I mumbled, as my mind threw out all reasonable thought processes and prepared to fully enter De Luca worship mode.

"I believe," he whispered in my ear, "that you were the one who brought sex into this conversation."

Then his finger moved, a strong motion that pushed aside my thong and thrust into my sex. I gasped, throwing back my head and pushed greedily down on his hand. A second finger joined the first, and they moved in perfect succession, fully inside and crooking inside of me, delicious swipes that had my eyes rolling back in ecstatic delirium. I reached out my hands, gripping his legs and squeezing, needing some type of grounding solidity to bring me back to reason.

His arms held me still, one wrapped around my pelvis and ending at the wet burial between my legs, the other holding my back tightly against his chest, the forearm hard against my stomach, the hand traveling from breast to breast, squeezing, teasing, and worshipping my tender skin.

It was coming, my core contracting around his fingers, my body arching against him. "Brad," I gasped, "I need ..."

He knew what I needed, and tightened his arms, holding me still, his upper hand turning whisper soft on my nipples as he increased the magic of his lower hand, his fingers taking me over the this-can't-be-fucking-happening mountain, and I fell, in a beautiful, free cascade, a full-body explosion of perfection that had me screaming his name, my words disappearing in the loud club music, my screams turning to moans, until I finally settled on a bed of Brad, my body spent and drunk against his, his fingers maintaining movement inside of me, taking me to a perfect, delirious ending until I collapsed.

***

We stayed in that moment, his fingers inside of me, my body heavy on his for a minute. Then, his hands and arms moved, my body curling as they brought me into a fetal position sideways in his lap. I leaned my head back against his arm, my eyes closed and mouth curving into a smile, loving the strength and security in his grip. I closed my eyes, at peace for a moment, until the unrelenting cock beneath my body shifted. It lacked social graces, the couth to understand that it was interrupting my post-orgasm bliss. It wanted only one thing: attention.

I laughed, meeting Brad's eyes, intense and mischievous all at one moment. "You got me all excited," he murmured, pulling me to him and stealing a kiss. "Surely you won't leave him hanging."

I looked out at the club, only lighting and walls a spectator to our alcove. Then I looked down, over the railing, my eyes dancing over sex at every turn. Not actual intercourse, but it was sex all the same, a flowing river of it, invading every pore, molecule, and breath of the downstairs space. An arched body, offering itself, in full glory, on stage. Lips against ears, whispered fantasies dancing between bodies. Spinning flesh, confidence via shot glass, sequins over tans, hands sliding over thighs, gripping ass, grabbing ankles. The sex crept up the walls, invaded the air, moved like invisible smoke upward, slithering into a hypnotic cloud into our room, curling around six feet two inches of sexuality. And underneath my body, legs spread, eyes potent, hardness impressively pushing up from below, was what I craved.

I moved, untangling from his arms and straddled him, sliding my dress upward, over my hips. His hands stopped me. "Let me," he said, taking over the action, his hands drawing out the process, firm fingers teasing as they pulled the dress over my body. The fabric came over my head, and I emerged to find his eyes on mine, intensity in them, his hands traveling slowly back down, a hand taking each breast and cupping them, his thumbs moving over my nipples lightly. "You know, I will never need anything more than you," he said softly. He sat up, a strong hand sliding around my back and lifting me easily, my body now suspended over him, my breasts soft cushions around his mouth. I moaned, his lips finding their way over the soft mounds and peaks of my breasts, hard flicks of his tongue against sensitive places, gentle scrapes of teeth following his soft mouth. His fingers dove back into that wet apex, moving in and out, readying me, moving my body into place until I felt his head. *There*. And he thrust, softly, only the head inside of me. His hand, cupping my ass, carrying my weight, kept me in place as he moved slowly, with short strokes, just his thick head dipping in and out of my folds.

"Brad," I murmured. "Please." Even as I spoke the words, I didn't mean them, didn't want him to stop. It was too perfect, too precise. Enough to enslave, too good to release, but not enough to fully satisfy. I didn't want satisfaction just yet. I wanted this, this incredible yearning met halfway, as a delicious crescendo of tongue and teeth danced across my breasts.

"I mean it, Julia," he groaned, lifting his mouth off me, stubble brushing roughly over my nipples.

Slow. Teasing. Strokes. Not. Far. Enough.

"Please, Brad. I need more," I gasped, gripping his hair, pulling his head back so I could look wildly into his eyes.

He lowered me marginally, his eyes locked in mine, his mouth forming words I didn't understand. "I don't need other woman, or to watch you with other men. What I need, all I need, is this."

He thrust, taking me fully, three rock-my-world strokes before withdrawing, his hand lifting me slightly, resuming his slow, half-inside strokes that left me whimpering in his arms. I was so close, could feel the orgasm coming despite his short strokes, a mounting pleasure that I held on to with determination. And then it swelled, my muscles tightening as one, building intensity that was taking me closer … closer ….

He stopped, his arms lifting me, my head snapping down, and my eyes flipping open. "What?" I gasped. "Why did you stop?"

"Not yet, Julia." He smiled, his cock taking one quick dip inside of me before withdrawing.

"Not *yet*? I'll come again, trust me." I pushed against his hand, frantic to maintain the momentum that I could feel slipping away.

He ignored me, cupping a breast with his free hand, and taking it into his mouth, his eyes glancing up and meeting my furious ones.

As fucking hot as it looked, his gorgeous face below me, my body in his mouth, my orgasm was waving goodbye, cheerily content with hopping in a minivan and hitchhiking to Cleveland. I gritted my teeth and grabbed his chin, pushing his face up to mine.

"Fuck me," I gritted out. "Now. Hard. Fast. De Luca-style."

He grinned, that sexy, I-fucking-own-you grin and released my ass, dropping me full force on top of my full-time obsession. Gripping me with both hands, he kept me still, and started a full on barrage from underneath. Hard, fast fucks that rammed my body, my core clenched against him, the pleasure erupting with every thrust from below, every hard pelvis hit against my clit. I moaned, over and over, the orgasm pulling a one-eighty and barreling full force toward me with arms extended wide. Harder, faster than it had ever come, my body a time bomb about to explode.

Then I did. Throwing my head back, my feet searching and finding floor, my hands grasping widely for anything to hold on to, I came, a full-body explosion that expelled every emotion I had contained for the last twenty-two years of my life. It was intense, it was incredible, and the best part was looking down on him as I finished, down into that cocky, sexual face that owned me with his eyes.

He thought I owned him. He thought he loved me, that I was enough. But this animal, this sex god who could drive me crazy and steal my heart in the same breath, he would never be fully mine. It was impossible. No one ever owned a god.

I took over control, pushing him back against the chair, digging my heels into the floor and riding his cock, my voice coming out in short bursts, guttural and raw as I took him closer to orgasm. "You say that now, but wait. Wait until you see me on top of another man. Wait 'til his arms are wrapped around my body, his mouth on my tits." I stared into his eyes, watched the dark flash of excitement as his hands traveled over my skin, possessively squeezing. "I'm going to come so hard on his cock, I'm going to fuck him until he explodes all over my sweet little face, and you're going to wonder, baby. You're going to wonder who made me come harder, whose cock I am thinking about next time you fuck me." He groaned and leaned forward, wrapping his arms around me, my breasts tight against his shirt, and came, thrusting into me, over and over, our juices mixing as he fucked me through the orgasm, his breath hot on my neck, his mouth taking mine until we both collapsed, spent and euphoric, on the leather chair.

No, no one ever owned a god. But I was working on taming, fooling him into submission.

candles.

oil.

touch.

temptation.

I awoke to an empty hotel room, the pillow top absent one impressively large body. Rolling over, I stretched, my arms reaching empty space instead of hard muscle. I frowned, propping up on one elbow and glanced at the clock. 11:13 a.m.

"Good morning, sleeping beauty." Brad strode in the room, rolling up the sleeves on a button-down shirt, looking ridiculously hot with a five-o-clock shadow and dress pants.

"What's all … this?" I gestured sleepily, my hand waving about in an attempt to include his head-to-toe hotness.

"What?" He frowned at me.

"You know what. You. All sexual."

"I was going to hit the tables before heading to Saffire."

"In that?" I sat fully upright.

He tilted his head at me, leaning back against the dresser and crossing his arms. "Yes. What's the problem?"

"You are, in a sense, breaking up with Alexis. Looking hot isn't going to help matters."

"You're being unreasonable. I didn't pack a lot of things, Julia. We came for one night."

I sputtered, moving off of the bed and walking over to him, my new vantage point making the effect only more potent. "Then buy something at the gift shop. A furry sweater, pleated jeans."

"What are you worried about?"

"Nothing," I mumbled, waving my arms and sighing dramatically. "Go on. I'll be fine here."

He bent, both hands gripping my waist and lifting me easily, my feet and arms flaying out as I struggled. Tossing me onto the bed he leaned over me, his face inches from mine. "Phillipe was going to set up some spa services. I assumed you'd want a massage."

I rolled my eyes, turning my face to the side. "Among other things."

"Want me to take care of you before I go downstairs?"

"No. I'll have Phillipe get me a masseuse that can pull double duty." I rolled over, burying my face in the pillow and trying to blot out the image of Brad's deliciousness in front of a sultry Alexis.

There was a pause, and I felt his presence moving closer. Then his hand brushed my hair aside, and his mouth was in my ear. "Be careful what you wish for, sweetheart. You should know that would only excite me."

I ignored him, ignoring the sweep of his fingertips along the nape of my neck. The trail of his finger down my back in one slow drag. I grinned against the sheet, desire curling in my belly as he dragged the sheet lower, exposing my back to the cool room. I felt his lips, soft broken up with the scruff of his stubble, on my back as he gave me a gentle kiss. Then he was gone, the suite door opening and closing with quiet finality.

***

I was in trouble the moment my name was spoken. I was half-asleep, cold cucumber on my eyes, a robe wrapped around my naked body, reclining in one of the suite's soft leather chairs. My hand was held by a spa attendant, the final adjustments being made to my manicure. Two women had transformed my hotel room into a spa, putting soothing tones on the Bose radio, closing the curtains, and dimming the lights to an appropriate level. While I normally would have gotten services in the spa downstairs, this time — given our short timeframe — Brad had arranged the services to be done in our suite. Through the muted sounds of wind and rain, I heard my name and opened my eyes.

He was beautiful in all of the ways that Brad wasn't. Thin where Brad was thick, blond hair where his was black. A tight polo that showed muscular arms, blue eyes that stared confidently out at me from a rugged face. *Yum.* I glanced down, tightening my robe and stood, sliding bare feet into slippers, padding gently across the stone floor 'til I stood in front of him.

"I've set up the table in the bedroom. Are you ready?" the man asked, a hint of California surfer in his tone.

I nodded, and he gestured for the door, holding it open as I moved through into a dim room, lit candles littering the space.

"I'll give you privacy," he spoke from behind me. "Please lie face up on the table. If you need me, just call out. My name is Tyler." I glanced over to him, nodding, my eyes catching the movement of the other attendants, their quiet and respectful departure as they left the suite. Then, the bedroom door closed, and I was alone.

I shed the robe, suddenly too aware of my nakedness, of his presence on the other side of the door. Candles filled the room with lavender and vanilla scents and danced flickering shadows over my skin. I laid on the table, pulling the sheet up to my chest, and then lowered myself until I was flat, my breasts tickled by the soft fabric, my head encased in a soft pillow. I closed my eyes and waited nervously for him to return.

Why was I nervous? Massages, once a foreign treat, had become commonplace in my new life of luxury. My body had been accustomed to strange hands, to men and women alike oiling up my body, to nudity a hairbreadth from gentle touches. I should be calm, relaxed, and ready for a treatment I have had fifty times before. But I wasn't. I was tense. Jittery. Wet. *Why the hell am I wet?* The panicked question flitted through my mind at the same time as I heard him enter.

The sound of the door first. It opened, then soft steps, the pad of feet against carpet, a sound I had to strain to hear. When he spoke, I flinched, my nerves a bundle of live wires. "Do you have any sensitive areas? Or places you'd like me to focus on?" He spoke softly, the husky tone sending a shiver through my body.

Sensitive areas? *A few.* Places I'd like him to focus on? *Yes, please.* "No. Just a normal Swedish massage, please." My voice behaved, coming out casually and unaffected, the right amount of offhand decorating its syllables.

"I understand. Mr. De Luca left very particular instructions," he said the words with a hint of seduction, his sentence causing my eyes to open.

Particular instructions from Brad? That could be worrisome. His earlier threat echoed in my mind. *Be careful what you wish for …* I had wished, hopefully he hadn't granted.

I let out a quiet breath. Willed my body to loosen, willed my tense muscles to stop telegraphing my stress. Why was this so difficult? Maybe I could blame it on the fact that we were in a bedroom instead of a spa. But more likely it was the tan Adonis whose hands were feeling a little too perfect. *Mr. De Luca left very particular instructions.* Trouble. I was definitely in trouble.

My nervousness melted a little with his movements, confident strokes of sensuality, attending to safe areas: my hands, forearms, and biceps. When he moved higher, I tensed; his hands kneaded me back to butter, his focus on my neck and shoulders. He slid his hands into my hair, used his fingers to massage and release tension. I exhaled, my lips parting slightly, and he traveled, a scent of candlewood and eucalyptus trailing behind him, and ended up at my feet, starting at my soles and working upward.

Ten minutes later I fully relaxed, still on my back, almost asleep, almost convinced that this was a standard service and not some fantasy come true, when his hands started their massage of my upper thighs. The sheet was tucked tightly around my body, and the flow of his hands over and around my thighs created a small puff of wind under the sheet, hitting my bare and waiting sex. It was a reminder, suddenly alerting me that I was, in fact, naked, his hands inches away, nothing but air between them and me. He moved higher, his hands separating, one on each thigh, and he slid them upward, dipping slightly under the sheet before continuing — his hands on top of the sheet.

I breathed easier, having the sheet between us — a barricade of sorts, and one that should keep my sinful thoughts at bay. His hands traveled, two palms across my body and then, I lost my breath.

They moved, in practiced, perfect paths, skimming across my breasts, the sheet underneath his hands only an additional weapon in the game of seduction. My nipples responded, instantly hardening, every light sweep of his hands a throb to my lower half. They swept, twin weapons of passion, down the sides of my stomach, the sheet dragging a little with them, hands moving back and forth, from breast to hip, a delicious sweep that moved a little lower with every pass, my pussy tightening in response, the thin sheet sticking to the moisture between my legs. I fought my pelvis, which, with each stroke of his hand, seemed to tip upward, trying to shorten the length and allow his fingers to reach my sex.

His hands slowed, his strokes shortened, and then, to my utter dismay, stopped.

"Ms. Campbell, if you could flip over, I will start on your back." His voice was professionally calm, an embarrassment, since I was at the point of practically gasping with need.

Flip over? Are you fucking kidding me? "Sure. That's fine." Miraculously, I didn't sound like a wanton slut, barely hanging on to her sanity. I sounded almost, practically, normal.

"Thank you, Ms. Campbell."

I turned over carefully, and he repositioned the sheet, exposing my back.

"You're so tense," he whispered, running his hand down the scoop of my back, his hands fanning out along the curve of my ass.

Shocker. I tried to relax, letting out a breath that ended up sounding like a moan. A sexual moan. *Fuck.*

He massaged, slow circles along my spine before making long swipes of his hands from one side of my back to the other. Traveling up along my back, he moved closer and closer to the sensitive skin along the side of my breasts. He slowed his movements, his fingertips grazing the outer swells of my breasts, my breath hitching despite myself.

Oh my God. I was getting wetter. I was naked, underneath the cool sheet, and could feel the moisture pooling between my legs, threatening to drip from my shaved lips. This was so bad, and I did some kegels, trying desperately to stop my body from reacting to his touch.

This was bad. This was bad in one of those ways where bad was good, and I didn't know if I wanted to be bad, or if I was even being bad if I followed temptation. Temptation was currently running his fingers slowly up my ribcage — my body still facedown. Temptation was now gently tracing the side of my breast, and I let out a moan despite myself.

The masseuse's fingers stopped their tease over my back and moved, trailing down the edge of my side, growing more aggressive as they reached the bottom of the sheet, dipping slightly underneath the fabric before gripping it.

Then he spoke, his voice unexpected in the candlelight darkness. "Ms. Campbell, may I remove the sheet?"

I swallowed, trying to bring some moisture to my dry mouth, then spoke, all offhanded casualness gone. "Yes. Please."

He tugged on the sheet drawing it slowly down the length of my lower half, every inch of exposure one more step down the staircase of desire. Then, it was off, my ass and body fully exposed to him, and I heard his breath quicken in the quiet bedroom.

With his question, with my response, I had given more than just permission to remove the sheet. I had opened the door, and I was slightly terrified about what would walk through it.

I lay on my stomach, my head on the pillow, grateful for the hide of my face, the layer of protection it, like my blindfold, gave. He started at my feet, behaving, normal kneading movements that shouldn't have been sexual, shouldn't have made my heart race and my pussy wet. Then he gently lifted and moved, one leg and then the other, spreading my legs slightly, the cold air of the room hitting my folds, alerting me to the fact that I was exposed, open to his eyes. His hands ran along my calves, oiling up my skin, his touch incredible on my tense muscles. I wondered how much he could see, if the moisture glistened between my legs. He worked silently, his touch slow enough to be sensual, practiced enough to be effective. I should have been relaxed, my muscles putty in his hands, but the fight to stay unaffected was only making me more aware. Aware of my open legs, aware of his strong hands, his masculine presence, the fact that I was naked before him. What would I do when it was time to turn over?

He moved closer, his hands sliding over the back of my knees and starting a slow, leisurely knead of my thighs, his large hands running and gripping their whole width, each movement insanely close to *me*, to the spot between my legs that was now soaked.

His hands stopped, releasing me, and he moved, coming around my body, my eyes opening and watching shadows pass until I felt his hands on my opposite side, taking the movement there. I closed my eyes, trying to relax, willing my muscles to loosen. I tried to concentrate on my breathing, tried to think about anything but the ten fingers that were inching their way up my thighs.

A hand touched my back, sliding up the curve of my spine until it reached the back of my neck. I frowned, my eyes opening, trying to understand the placement of the hand, and the location of the masseuse, my bombarded brain confused, then realizing the impossibility of the situation, the impossibility of three hands on one man, and I stiffened, starting to rise, but feeling the hand on my neck keep me down.

"Relax." Brad's voice was in my ear, his hand turning from strong to caressing in moments. "It's me." I obeyed, my body instantly releasing the tension, his presence reassuring to my nervous body. My limbs became loose, and the masseuse's hands continued their perfect manipulation of my thighs. He nuzzled my ear, placing a quick kiss on my neck. "Do you want him to continue, or should I ask him to leave?"

I took a deep breath, knowing the answer before he even finished the question. "Continue."

He chuckled in my ear, his mouth finding my neck again before he straightened. "I'll be here, baby."

Knowing he was there, in the room, in control of the situation, allowed me to fully enjoy Tyler's touch. I inched my legs farther apart, and felt his touch change, the gain of confidence and control with the additional permission. He spread his fingers, the same strokes of my upper thigh now barely brushing my velvet folds, the soft sporadic contact driving me absolutely wild. I had never had so much buildup, so much teasing without fulfillment, and I had an ache that was running out of control. I arched my back, lifting my ass up, reaching, trying to get more, but he kept me at bay, kept his hands on my thighs, the only solace in the occasional brush that seemed almost accidental in its contact.

I heard Brad move, my ears attuned to every sound, the clunk of his watch as he unclipped it and dropped the heavy item on the dresser. His belt, the slide of leather through cloth as he removed it. Leather creaking as he settled into the chair in the corner of the room.

The hands on my body separated, now one on each thigh, and the man moved beyond the professional borders, running gentle hands down the skin of my inner thigh, then a soft hand over my sex, gently passing up and down my lips. I whimpered, holding back a beg, gripping the side of the table and fighting the urge to turn over and demand more.

"Flip over," Brad's voice spoke from the corner.

I complied, moving carefully on the narrow bed, lifting up, my vision suddenly open, my eyes taking in the room. Brad settled comfortably in the chair, one leg up on an ottoman, his dress shirt untucked, possession in his eyes. The masseuse, still fully dressed while I laid there naked, on display for the two men in the room.

"Proceed, Tyler."

I relaxed my head, closing my eyes, and was surprised to feel the silk of the sheet, settling back over my body, my nakedness covered once again. The man spoke respectfully, his voice above me. "Should I continue what I was doing earlier?"

I nodded. "Please." Inside, I was screaming the word, my sub-conscious dragging herself up his thighs, shaking with excitement as she clapped with greedy hands.

It was the same as before, but different, my body so ready, no needy, that every touch was electrified. The knowledge of where Brad was, the possession in his eyes, the knowledge that he was watching, compounded my arousal. The masseuse continued, resuming his movement, his hands caressing as they moved, up and over the swell of my breasts, then back down the side of my stomach. The heat of a hand against a cool sheet, my skin both hating and loving the material, all at the same time. The push and pull of the fabric as his hand moved, brushing against my nipples when he was pressing down along my stomach, tugged at the place where I was wet on his journey upward. Up and down, each swipe seeming to move down, but so teasingly slow I was wondering if it was all in my imagination. The sheet shifted, one hand definitely lower, taking the sheet with it, and I felt cool air slip along one breast, the nipple close to exposure. Up. Down. Closer, but not there. My nipples tender, alive with stimulation. My pussy crying, begging for attention and touch.

Then, his movements were finally long enough, and I felt his hand slide slowly downward until it completely covered my sex.

Brad was watching, but not participating. *Is this cheating? Is this allowed?* Alarm bells rang in my head, but I was unable to listen, a need so great pulsing between my legs, his hand moving slightly as he pulled it away, north along my body, and then back downward. The sheet between us was now soaked, one hand passing aggressively, then softly, then aggressively, down between my legs, the other hand moving back and forth along my breasts, strumming my nipples, my body beginning to arch from his touch. Fuck rules and commitments, anything sane or rational. Brad wasn't going to open my sexual boundaries, send this madness in, and not expect me to fucking enjoy it. I moaned, the sound loud and begged, my lips parting, my eyes opening, and I propped myself up, the sheet falling from my breasts, and stared into the masseuse's eyes.

"I need you to fuck me. Now." I gasped the words, my mouth hanging open, the cold air against erect nipples, his hand cupping me, and one finger moved, swiping under the sheet; he slid it inside of me, and my world went dark.

My arms gave out, and I fell back, arching, a second finger joining the first, and he moved them together, his other hand sliding the sheet farther down, baring my upper half, my body offered to him as I pushed against his hand. He curved his fingers, stroking my g-spot, his other hand worshipping my breasts, now lifting, squeezing and then the additional stimulation of his mouth, hot and wet, sucking and pulling me against his tongue. I reached out, gripping his shirt, my eyes squeezed shut and bucked, my orgasm flooding uncontrolled, an explosion of De Luca proportions. He kept up the movement, my other hand reaching out and finding his shoulder, holding on for dear life as my body let out a final shudder, and then I collapsed on the bed, aftershocks twitching like erratic tics through my body.

My eyes closed, and I heard footsteps travel, latches click, the door open, and then shut. I opened my eyes, turning my head until I could see Brad, at my side, his eyes on my body. I watched him, watched as he placed a hand lightly on my ribcage, running it down my body as he circled the table, his eyes traveling along my skin, an intent, brooding look mixed in with his possessive standard. I murmured, a soft tone of satisfaction that had his eyes looking to mine, the corners of his mouth twitching slightly as he rounded the end of the table and stopped beside me. Bending over, he slid his arms under my body and stood, cradling me to his chest, my body curving, and I instinctively leaned into him, inhaling his scent, one that was 100% Brad, a smile crossing my face when I smelled only him on his shirt and neck. He carried me to the bed, lying me down on the pillow top, my face turning to him as he stood next to the bed, looking down at me.

"Did you enjoy that?"

I nodded, my eyes closing softly, a small smile on my lips. "Why'd he leave?"

He chuckled. "I can bring him back if you'd like. Call and get a later flight."

"What time is it?"

He glanced at the bedside table. "Almost 4:45."

My eyes opened fully, and I pushed off the bed. "Shit! We've got to go."

He pressed me back down, black need in his eyes. "Not yet," he said, unbuttoning his pants. "Not yet."

***

Sex with Brad was always different after a threesome. Sometimes it was tender, such as when we were with the Russian girl. Other times it was possessive, as if he was claiming me back, reasserting his dominance with his cock, hands, and mouth. And sometimes it was fire, two souls battling each other, passion and fury in between our bodies, the giant need for each other frenzied in its intensity.

That day, with precious minutes ticking by, I expected it to be fast. But he took his time, laying me back on the bed, his eyes moving slowly over my skin, drinking me in. His hands dropping his pants, then his underwear, until there was nothing but raw, hard cock. Ready for me. Wanting me. He leaned over my body, tasted with teasing kisses, my neck, breasts, the side of my stomach, the curve of my hip. His hands pulled my legs open, and I squirmed as he drug soft lips closer, along the cut where my panties would lie, his eyes catching mine as he lowered his mouth to my sex.

God. I bucked under his mouth. His tongue was a velvet soft flutter over my sensitive clit. I was so aroused. On the edge of everything. He took me to the peak, keeping the rhythm up until I cried his name and clenched my legs. Until I came, my back arching, my hands finding and gripping his thick hair.

He moved up my body, joining me on the bed, his knees pushing my legs apart, his cock settling and thrusting into my hot and ready core.

"Are you mad?" I whispered, staring into his face.

He cocked his head at me, confused.

"At what he was doing … when you came in."

He chuckled, shoved fully in, a place he didn't typically go, the extreme depth of him usually painful. I winced, slapped his chest, warning him with my eyes. "I'm only mad if he was doing something you didn't want. or, if he was making you uncomfortable. From the looks of it, you were very comfortable."

"But you didn't mind just watching?"

"Watching you being pleased?" He shook his head, dragged his hips backward, then gripped my legs and pushed back in. "Seeing your face when you come, your muscles when they clench. The arch of your back at a time when I can focus on it, enjoy it. I lose so many sensations when I fuck you. Your sounds, the flush of your cheeks. Sitting there, watching you come … it was the most beautiful thing I have ever seen. It's not about 'minding.' It's about enjoying." He quickened his thrusts, the movements of his hips, and dropped my legs, returned to my mouth. Then he wrapped his arms underneath me, pulled me to his chest, and rolled us over, our bodies joined as one, until I was astride, and he was below. And then he gave me a brief moment of control, and let me ride him to completion.

"Show her," he said. "Show her how you suck my cock."

Brad smiled. It had been a good birthday. No mess, no fuss, no drama. A great dinner at Centaur with the woman who had stolen his heart. And now, home. Before, it had been simply a house, a place where he bedded women, ate Martha's cooking, and slept. Now, with Julia's light and warmth and messy adorableness, it had become more. He had begged, bribed, and seduced — all in an attempt to get her to move in. But she had stubbornly resisted, returning most nights to the hovel she called a home. And every night she slept away from him, he worried. He unlocked the door, disengaging the alarm, and felt the presence of her pass behind him, her hands flicking on lights as her heels clicked through the kitchen.

She moved perfectly, his eyes following her steps, the curves of her body underneath her dress, her shapely legs on perfect display atop sexy heels. He locked the door and caught up to her as she rounded the corner, heading for the stairs.

"Whoa," he whispered into her neck, inhaling the scent of her as his hands wrapped around her waist and traveled up the front of her dress. His mouth nuzzled her neck and planted soft kisses on her fragrant skin.

"Brad," she whispered, spinning from him and walking backward toward the stairs. "You can finish that upstairs."

"I can't wait that long," he said gruffly, catching her hand and pulling her tightly to him. He lowered his mouth to hers, silencing her response, his hands tugging on the straps of her dress quickly, the material following the path of the straps, her lace-covered breasts quickly exposed to his hands. She groaned, her chest heaving once underneath his mouth, her hands pushing on his chest.

"Stop," she said breathlessly, pulling up her dress until her perfect breasts were once again hidden. "Just wait a sec. I need something from upstairs."

Before he could formulate a response, she was gone, the flash of red soles moving quicker than humanly possible up the staircase. He followed closely, his eyes on the curve of her ass. He grinned, reaching a hand up to grab her when he reached the landing and everything stopped at the sight of two men.

***

I heard Brad behind me, getting closer, and I could tell you without looking that he would be reaching for me, intent on getting his hands on some part of my body. I felt triumphant when I reached the top landing untouched, and moved toward the guest room, my smile acknowledging the men that sat outside the door. Brad's voice stopped me instantly, his tone one I had never heard from him. "Julia. Go into the safe room." I froze mid-step and turned to him.

His eyes were not on me, but on the two suits, the large bodyguards who flanked either side of the guest room door, seated in the two casual chairs that typically occupied the sitting area of the guest room. I instantly understood his concern and cursed my own lack of foresight. The two men rose at Brad's tone, their stance one of combative preparation.

I moved three steps, until I stood in front of Brad and blocked his line of sight. His eyes flickered to me briefly, clouds of worry. "Brad, it's okay. I called them here. They are fine." My words took a moment to register, his eyes watching them instead of me, but then confusion crossed his handsome face, and his eyes met mine again.

I smiled, placing my hands gently on his chest and kissed his cheek. "Relax," I whispered. Then I turned, stepping through the men and to the guest room, where I swung the door open wide for Brad's eyes.

The room was dim but not dark, a big enough room that the bed was set back against a far wall, the lit candles revealing enough: glowing skin, blonde hair, porcelain features – the package lounged atop a cream duvet. Brad's frame relaxed a fraction, and he glanced at the men with new understanding, then his gaze settled on my face, a look of confusion affecting his features in an adorable way I had never seen.

"Happy birthday," I whispered and walked ahead of him, into the dark room, unzipping my dress as I walked.

***

There was a click, and I turned to see Brad shut the door, his eyes slowly sweeping over me, surveying the bed, his eyes dark and unreadable. Then they returned to me, and he moved only one step forward, his hands pulling off his jacket, tossing it aside, then moving to his belt, the slow, deliberate unbuckling of leather causing my breath to hitch.

A million thoughts ran through my head. *What do I do? Do I get on the bed with her? Approach him? Sit in the chair?*

"Turn around." Brad stepped closer, his eyes on mine, the pull of his stare too great to break, and I turned my back to him slowly, hating to break the eye contact.

His hand swept down my bare back, pulling my zipper farther, to the place I couldn't take it, his hands spreading the dress over my shoulders and letting it fall to the floor. "Keep the heels on," he muttered.

"Do you want me to watch?" I said the words softly, looking over my shoulder at him. I was almost afraid of the answer. Afraid because even I didn't even know what I wanted. I glanced at the girl still on the bed, her body stretched, on her side, expression quiet, eyes open. Watching. Our eyes met and she smiled. A friendly, reassuring expression. *It will be okay. Trust me.*

He shook his head. "I'm not ever, as long as I live, going to have an orgasm without your hand on my cock, your mouth on my lips. If you want to bring in another girl, that is fine. But you are not watching. I'm not settling for second best when you are here." He ran his hand down my back, his hand leaving my skin for a moment before coming back to my ass with one, firm slap, the sensation catching me off guard, and I jumped, turning my head to him, caught off guard by the dark yet playful look in his eyes. "Now get on the bed before you are the death of me."

I smiled shyly at the girl as I climbed upon the bed, her long limbs rolling over as she crawled to her knees, making room. She reached out a tentative hand, running it softly over my skin, the touch so foreign, so soft and delicate. "You are beautiful," she whispered, her hand trailing over and across my back and down my arm.

"So are you."

There was the metal sound of a buckle, and I turned to see Brad unzipping his pants, his shirt removed, his weight joining us on the bed as he knee-walked forward, settling back into pillows, sliding in between us. "Come here, baby," he said. "Straddle me."

I did, my ass settling into the hard bridge of his stomach, his head tilting up to look into my eyes. "You didn't need to do this."

"I wanted to," I said softly, running my hands up the hard muscles of his chest.

"I get off pleasing you, watching you pleased. Another girl … I don't want this if you don't enjoy it."

"I want to try it. We can discuss the rest later."

"Just look at me if you are uncomfortable. I'll know. I'll stop." His hand played with the small of my back before curving down and squeezing my ass. "You nervous?"

I laughed, the question releasing some of my tension. "A little."

"Don't be. This is just like the others." He sat up slightly, his arms wrapping around my waist, his mouth laying a kiss against my neck. "It's about you and pleasure."

I pushed him down, not liking where this was going. "No. This is about your birthday, and rocking your old man world."

He laughed, letting me push him, settling back against the pillows. "Easy, baby. You can't call me an old man on my birthday. And," he said, his voice darkening, "you're doing a lot of ordering around considering it's my birthday. Kiss me."

I pursed my lips, shot him a look I knew he loved, one that spat fire and conceded defeat, and leaned back down, caught off guard when he captured my hands and pulled them together behind me, his large hand easily pinning them to my back.

"What's her name?" he asked, his mouth inches from mine.

"January."

"January, pull out my cock, please."

I squirmed slightly, caught off guard by his directive, his hand tight on my wrists, keeping me in place. I felt her move, heard the rustle of fabric, the buck of Brad underneath me as he lifted his ass to assist her. He kissed me, his free hand firm on the back of my head, his tongue making a statement that was both strong and needy.

He pulled on my wrists, sitting up with me, my ass sliding down, bumping against her hand and his cock. "Hop off." He released my wrists, moving his hands to my breasts and pushing them into his mouth, taking one frantic taste of them before moving me off.

"Show her," he said. "Show her how you suck my cock."

I knelt on the other side of his body, admiring the thick lay of his cock on his stomach, her hand sliding up and down his thighs. I glanced up, watching her kneel across from me, her blue eyes down, glued to Brad, and I felt a moment of pride as I reached forward, gently lifting and taking his semi-hard cock into my mouth, feeling it stiffen as I sucked, my throat closing, my eyes watering slightly as I took as much of him as I could. I worked his shaft with my hand, sucking hard, watching as January moved a hand forward, running her hands over his balls, then leaned forward, taking them in her mouth.

I felt Brad's hand on my hair, gathering it up in his fist, pushing and pulling it gently, his eyes on mine, his mouth opening slightly as he scowled with concentration, watching his cock as it slid in and out of my mouth. He was so hard, so slick and thick in my mouth, and I watched his eyes close briefly as I took him as far down as I could. "Jesus, baby," he groaned. "You are so perfect."

I drug slowly off his cock, meeting January's eyes, and she took over, her mouth smoothly picking up where mine had left off. Brad's hand, still in my hair, tugged gently, and I looked over, letting him pull me up his body until I was tucked into his arm, his mouth on mine, his other hand taking a tour of my chest, squeezing and pulling each breast in turn, his hands a little rough in their journey. My mouth gasped against his as he slapped each breast slightly, the arm underneath me shifting as he slid his left hand lower, until it cupped my ass, his fingers splaying over and teasing my pussy, the sensitive skin of my taint, and my ass. I moaned, pushing against his hand, wanting more, my mouth pulling off his as I lifted my head and watched her, watching the strange girl take his cock with skill. I could see how hard he was, see the light pink dart of her tongue, the hot interior of her mouth, the veins on his cock —

Fuck.

My eyes closed, two of Brad's fingers sliding into me, one in the hot, tight hole of my ass, one in my wet cunt, the curve of his grip absolutely perfect, his second hand sliding down from my breasts and rubbing gently over my clit. Oh my God. It was incredible, having both of his hands stimulating me, his mouth on my neck, my eyes fighting to open, wanting to take in more of the experience, the arousal of watching him pleasured more than I expected.

I could feel the tightening in my stomach, the clench of my muscles that warned me an orgasm was coming. "Brad, I can't …" I closed my eyes, felt the nips of his teeth on my neck, the vibration of his throat when he growled.

"Come for me. Come for me while she sucks my cock."

I couldn't stop it; my hands gripped his arm like it was a safety bar, holding on tightly when my back arched, when the orgasm ripped through me like an out of control wind. I cursed his name, a string of obscenities pouring out of me as pleasure blossomed, his fingers softening perfectly as my body surrendered to the perfect peak and then fell into the pit of sensitivity. Then, my clit was left alone entirely, his mouth feasting on my neck as he did nothing but pulse his fingers inside of me, my ass clenching around him, the orgasm drawn further out, so much so that I wonder if I had two back-to-back.

Then I sunk, a mess of wanton pleasure in his arms, curled over, my face against his chest, his hands moving me into place without me even knowing it, the girl helping to slide my leg over his stomach until I was back, straddling him, this time him gripping my face in his hands, his face inches away, and he stared into my eyes.

I wanted to close my eyes, too weak with bliss to focus, but he held me firm, arrested me with his stare. I felt strange hands, delicate and soft, *hers*, running down the pucker of my ass, and then his cock, so fucking hard, was at my sex, and she was pushing it in, putting it into place.

Brad went wild.

I loved him fucking me from underneath. Loved the jack hammer of his cock as I did nothing, and he went eight kinds of crazy, the animalistic hunger of his fucks incredibly hot, adding fuel to an already blazing fire, my body loving the barrage on my cunt, the nonstop friction, the push and pull against my g-spot and deep in, quick out, deep in, quick out that drove me over the brink of orgasm in less than a minute.

I came hard, my entire body seizing, squeezing, the delicate push of her finger against my ass sending me straight into holy fuckville territory. It was long, it was insane, it was beautiful, staring into Brad's eyes, his mouth whispering words I could barely hear but knew by heart. "I love you. You crazy sexual beauty. I love every fucking inch of you. I love watching you. I love seeing you in this way. You are mine, you dirty, kinky woman."

Then I shoved off, amazed I still had strength in my body. I rolled off him and lay spent, my limbs useless, my heart pounding. "Fuck her," I moaned. "Please."

"On your knees," Brad ordered, the girl sliding over and assuming the position, her perfect ass bent over before him, my view of the *damn she's hot* scene enough to give me a moment's hesitation. But he moved her, turning her toward me, so that her face was skimming my stomach, her hot breath moving fluidly over my skin. He was positioned behind her, facing me, his eyes on mine, dark possession and arousal in his gaze, a condom package in hand, raised to his mouth for easy opening. Also in his eyes — a question. An 'are you ready for this?' inquiry. I nodded once, my eyes glued to his. He studied me for a second before he ripped the foil package open.

**

There had been a moment, when Brad had ordered her to her knees, when I was already two orgasms down, and she hadn't even been touched, that I felt bad for this woman. That I felt like we were using her, not respecting her properly. All of that left my mind when he moved inside of her. Didn't thrust, didn't shove. He took his time — let her adjust. One long, slow movement of his body forward. Her head dropped back, away from my body, and she let out a sound. Something in between a moan and a groan, a satisfied sound, which made me smile, my spent body reviving. Yes, I knew. I knew exactly what that felt like. The chemical reaction of his cock that was somehow, impossibly, different than any other man's. She wasn't getting him bare. She wasn't getting the full force of Brad De Luca. But even sheathed with latex, his cock was incredible. Then he started moving, started fucking, his hands falling to her ass, gripping, squeezing. He leaned slightly forward, gripped her skin, stared into my eyes and moved.

I got it. I got why he did this. I didn't think I'd ever need it the way he did, our threesomes his assurance that I was *beyond* satisfied. He didn't want just satisfaction from me. He wanted my mind ripped three ways from Sunday, wanted my body to peak and fall fifteen times in one night. Wanted me to feel raw animalism alongside heart-stopping passion. Wanted me to feel beautiful, sexual. Wanted me to open every padlocked closet in my fantasy palace and explore whatever treats I locked away. He would never be satisfied with ordinary, would never want just part of my heart, part of my body. He wanted every barrier stripped, every veil lifted, until he and I were fucking intertwined, my pleasure giving him his pleasure, his pleasure giving me mine.

I got it. The feeling that suddenly swelled through me. It was insanity in the form of raving, passionate lust. I felt competitive and jealous and sexual, all rolled into one. I knew, as I stared into his eyes, as he swept a greedy, ravenous stare over my body, that he wanted me. He was eating my body with his gaze, his fucks increasing in tempo, the girl's cries mounting as he stopped being gentle and started being Brad.

"Fuck yourself," he gritted out. "With your fingers. Let me see you. Let me see inside you."

I rolled over and moved back, until I was before them. I spread my legs, dipped a finger, then two, inside my mouth, Brad's eyes darkening as I sucked them. Not lightly, not with ladylike daintiness. I sucked my fingers and wanted his cock. I drug my wet fingers down, his stare following, the muscles on his chest and shoulders standing to attention as he drilled into her, and I spread my lips and let him see the extent of my arousal, the extent of my want.

She was close. I could hear the change in her cries, the slap of Brad's balls, each thrust spanking her clit, his rapid-fire motion taking her quickly up the hill of orgasm. My eyes left Brad's, watching her face, her expression. She met my gaze, her own almost frantic. Gone was the cool and collected vixen who waited on this bed, candles illuminating her perfect skin. Right then she was a current of *whatthefuckishappening*, an identity I knew well, her eyes glazing over as she lost all rational thought and exploded. My fingers stopped fucking around, stopped their teasing ways. They found their way to my sex and dove inside.

***

I thought I knew Julia but I didn't. There was so much I had yet to discover, yet to unearth. We hadn't talked about this, hadn't talked about bringing another woman into the bedroom. I didn't need it. It didn't feed my competitive fire. I didn't need to know that I was the best every woman out there has had. I only needed to be *her* best, only needed to learn every inch of *her* body and the way to light it on fire.

But did *she* need a girl? Did she have the same competitive fight that I carried? Did it get her off to see me fuck another woman? If so, I would bang away. Fuck this blonde when the woman I wanted was spread open before me, her fingers where my mouth or cock should be, her chest heaving with intensity that I was not causing.

My fear was that it was not for her. My fear was that she was doing this for me, thinking that this is something I needed, I wanted. My fear was that she hated this, and I was killing a piece of her sexual fire with every stroke into this stranger. I gave one final thrust and pulled out, squeezing the girl's ass and gently rolling her aside, bending forward until my mouth was on Julia, and I was tasting her sweet pussy. Her fingers moved for my mouth, her body bucked up and I grabbed her, held her down and used my tongue to tease the hell out of my future wife.

God, I loved this woman.

***

Brad took me to a third high, my barriers to orgasm
weak, each peak making the next one easier, my
body a tight coil of arousal. January's mouth
covered my breasts, her firm tongue playing against
my nipples, her teeth gentle when she grazed them
across my skin. I reached a hand out, brushed it
over her breasts, their weight heavy. They moved so
differently than mine. They hung when she bent
over, bounced when she got fucked. I tentatively
squeezed one, and she smiled, moved closer for
easier access. Kissed me softly as I explored her
upper half.

Then I came, and everything went black.

***

A fight of tongues. Both of us greedy for more. Of
his shaft, of his head, the small bit of pre-cum that
leaked from his tip. Occasionally our mouths would
meet, join for a moment of playful fun, then return,
our hands also on him. Stroking. Eyes begging. On
our knees on the soft carpet before him.

His never left mine. Dark intensity. Fierce arousal.
They stayed on me until his thighs clenched, his abs
tightened, his hand found the back of my head and

pulled me foremost on his cock. I dove, sucking hard, using my hand and staring up into his face. Then his mouth moved, my name as a groan on his lips and his eyes lidded shut.

I love watching him come.

I took what I could, and January's tongue chimed in, helping me drain him dry. Then he lifted us, one by one, to our feet.

"We'll leave you the room," he said. "Take as long as you need, the attached bath and shower is yours if you need it."

She didn't linger, and a few minutes later, with our passports back in the safe, the men and January gone, Brad closed the door to our bedroom, and fixed me with a look. A look I knew, yet still questioned.

"Get on the bed," he growled.

I didn't move fast enough, and he lifted me up, carrying me in four large strides to the bed where he tossed me, the robe I had thrown on tangling in my limbs, and I fought the silk and looked into his mischievous eyes. "What, you didn't like your present?"

"That wasn't my present," he said, bending over me, his mouth nuzzling the silk robe open, his hands untying the sash and spreading it, bites and kisses running down the length of my torso as he climbed atop the bed, my legs opening before him. "This. This will be my present."

I didn't know what man considered two hours of driving me wild a present, but I could tell you this—

I wasn't ever letting him go.

The erotic scenes in this book were pulled from three books:
The Dumont Diaries
Sex Love Repeat
End of the Innocence (Innocence #3)

My full list of published works:
Blindfolded Innocence (Innocence trilogy #1)
Masked Innocence (Innocence trilogy #2)
End of the Innocence (Innocence trilogy #3)
The Dumont Diaries
Sex Love Repeat
The Girl in 6E
Bend (an erotic anthology)

If this is your first taste of erotica, consider reading the full-length books, the sex becomes even hotter when you can attach emotions to the scenes.

Thank you for supporting my work. I appreciate it greatly.

xoxo,

Alessandra

About the Author

Alessandra Torre is a USA Today Bestselling author who focuses on contemporary erotica. Her first book, Blindfolded Innocence, was published in July 2012, and was an Erotica #1 Bestseller for two weeks.

Alessandra lives in Florida and is married to an alpha male who she can't get enough of. She enjoys reading, spending time with her family, and playing with her dogs. She publishes an average of four books a year.

Printed in Great Britain
by Amazon